THE MARAKAIOS MARRIAGE

THE MARAKAIOS MARRIAGE

BY

KATE HEWITT

First published in Great Britain 2015
by Mills & Boon, an imprint of Harlequin (UK) Limited,
Large Print edition 2015
Eton House, 18-24 Paradise Road,
Richmond, Surrey, TW9 1SR

ISBN: 978-0-263-25674-1

Harlequin (UK) Limited's policy is to use papers that are natural, renewable and recyclable products and made from wood grown in sustainable forests. The logging and manufacturing processes conform to the legal environmental regulations of the country of origin.

Printed and bound in Great Britain
by CPI Antony Rowe, Chippenham, Wiltshire

To Pippa Roscoe—thank you
for your invaluable feedback on this story.

CHAPTER ONE

'HELLO, LINDSAY.'

How could two such innocuous-sounding words cause her whole body to jolt, first with an impossible joy, and then with a far more consuming dread? A dread that seeped into her stomach like acid, corroding those few seconds of frail, false happiness as she registered the cold tone of the man she'd once promised to love, honour and obey.

Her husband, Antonios Marakaios.

Lindsay Douglas looked up from her computer, her hands clenching into fists in her lap even as her gaze roved helplessly, hungrily over him, took in his familiar features now made strange by the coldness in his eyes, the harsh downturn of his mouth. With her mind still spinning from the sight of him, she said the first thing that came into it.

'How did you get in here?'

'You mean the security guard?' Antonios sounded merely disdainful, but his whisky-brown eyes glowed like banked coals. 'I told him I was your husband. He let me through.'

She licked her dry lips, her mind spinning even as she forced herself to focus. Think rationally. 'He shouldn't have,' she said. 'You have no business being here, Antonios.'

'No?' He arched an eyebrow, his mouth curving coldly, even cruelly. 'No business seeing my wife?'

She forced herself to meet that burning gaze, even though it took everything she had. 'Our marriage is over.'

'I am well aware of that, Lindsay. It's been six months, after all, since you walked out on me without any warning.'

She heard the accusation in his voice but refused to rise to it. There was no point now; their marriage was over, just as she'd told him.

'I only meant that all the academic buildings are locked, with security guards by the door,' she answered. Her voice sounded calm—far calmer than she felt. Seeing Antonios again was causing memories to rise up in her mind like a flock of seagulls, crying out to her, making her remember things she'd spent the last six months determined to forget. The way he'd held her after they'd made love, how he'd always so tenderly tucked her hair behind her ears, cupped her cheek with his hand, kissed her eyelids. How happy and safe and cherished he'd once made her feel.

No, she couldn't remember that. Better to remember the three months of isolation and confusion she'd spent at his home in Greece as Antonios had become more and more obsessed with work, expecting her simply to slot into a life she'd found alien and even frightening.

Better to remember how depressed and despairing she'd felt, until staying in Greece for one more day, one more *minute*, had seemed impossible.

Yes, better to remember that.

'I still don't know why you're here,' she told him. She placed her hands flat on the desk and stood, determined to meet him at eye level, or as close as she could, considering he topped her by eight inches.

Yet just looking at him now caused her to feel a tug of longing deep in her belly. The close-cut midnight-dark hair. The strong square jaw. The sensual, mobile lips. And as for his body…taut, chiselled perfection underneath the dark grey silk suit he wore. She knew his body as well as her own. Memories rushed in again, sweet and poignant reminders of their one sweet week together, and she forced them away, held his sardonic gaze.

Antonios arched one dark eyebrow. 'You have no idea why I might be here, Lindsay? No reason to wonder why I might come looking for my errant wife?'

Errant wife. So he blamed her. Of course he did. And she knew he had a right to blame her, because she'd left him without an explanation or even, as he'd said, a warning. But he'd forced her to leave, even if he couldn't, or wouldn't, ever understand that. 'It's been six months, Antonios,' she told him coolly, 'and you haven't been in touch once. I think it's reasonable to be surprised to see you.'

'Didn't you think I'd ever come, demanding answers?'

'I gave you an answer—'

'A two-sentence email is not an explanation, Lindsay. Saying our marriage was a mistake without saying why is just cowardice.' He held up a hand to forestall her reply, although she couldn't think of anything to say. 'But don't worry yourself on that account. I have no interest in your explanations. Nothing would satisfy me now, and our marriage ended when you walked away without a word.'

Frustration bubbled through her and emotion burned in her chest. Maybe she hadn't had so many words when she'd finally left, but that was because she'd used them all up. Antonios hadn't heard any of it. 'The reason I'm here,' he continued, his voice hard and unyielding, 'is because I need you to return to Greece.'

Her jaw dropped and she shook her head in an instantaneous gut reaction.

'I can't—'

'You'll find you can, Lindsay. You pack a bag and get on a plane. It's that easy.'

Mutely she shook her head. Just the thought of returning to Greece made her heart start to thud hard, blood pounding in her ears. She focused on her breathing, trying to keep it even and slow. One of the books she'd read had advised focusing on the little things she could control, rather than the overwhelming ones she couldn't. Like her husband and his sudden return into her life.

Antonios stared at her, his whisky-brown eyes narrowed, his lips pursed, his gaze ruthlessly assessing. *In. Out. In. Out.* With effort she slowed her breathing, and her heart stopped thudding quite so hard.

She glanced up at him, conscious of how he was staring at her. And she was staring at him; she couldn't help herself. Even angry as he so obviously was, and had every right to be, he looked beautiful. She remembered when she'd first seen him in New York, with snowflakes dusting his hair and a whimsical smile on his face as he'd caught sight of her standing on Fifth

Avenue, gazing up at the white spirals of the Guggenheim.

I'm lost, he'd said. *Or at least I thought I was.*

But she'd been the one who had been lost, in so many ways. Devastated by the death of her father. Spinning in a void of grief and fear and loneliness she'd been trying so hard to escape.

And then she'd lost herself in Antonios, in the charming smile he'd given her, in the warmth she'd seen in his eyes, in the way he'd looked at her as if she were the most interesting and important woman in the world. For a week, a mere seven days, they'd revelled in each other. And then reality had hit, and hit hard.

'Let me clarify,' he said, his voice both soft and so very cold. 'You *will* come to Greece. As your husband, I command you.'

She stiffened. 'You can't *command* me, Antonios. I'm not your property.'

'Greek marriage law is a little different from American law, Lindsay.'

She shook her head, angry now, although not, she suspected, as angry as he was. 'Not that different.'

'Perhaps not,' he conceded with a shrug. 'But I am assuming you want a divorce?'

The sudden change in subject jolted her. 'A divorce...'

'That *is* why you left me, is it not? Because you no longer wished to continue in our marriage.' He bared his teeth in a smile and Lindsay suppressed the sudden urge to shiver. She'd never seen Antonios look this way. So cold and hard and predatory.

'I...' A divorce sounded so final, so terrible, and yet of course that had to be what she wanted. She'd left him, after all.

In the six months since she'd left Greece, she'd immersed herself in the comforting cocoon of number theory, trying to finish her doctorate in Pure Mathematics. Trying to blunt that awful ache of missing Antonios, or at least the Antonios she'd known for one week, before everything had changed. She'd tried to take steps to put her life back together, to control her anxiety and reach out to the people around her. She'd made progress, and there had been moments, whole days, when she'd felt normal and even happy.

Yet she'd always missed Antonios. She'd missed the person she'd been with him, when they'd been in New York.

And neither of those people had been real. Their marriage, their love, hadn't been real. She knew that absolutely, and yet…

She still longed for what they'd shared, so very briefly.

'Yes,' she said quietly. She lifted her chin and met his gaze. 'I want to end our marriage.'

'A divorce,' Antonios clarified flatly. Lindsay flinched slightly but kept his gaze, hard and unyielding as it was.

'Yes.'

'Then, Lindsay,' he told her in that awful silky voice, 'you need to do as I ask. *Command.* Because under Greek marriage law, you can't get a divorce unless both parties agree.'

She stared at him, her eyes widening as she considered the implications of what he was saying. 'There must be other circumstances in which a divorce is permissible.'

'Ah, yes, there are. Two, as a matter of fact.' His mouth twisted unpleasantly. 'Adultery and abandonment. But as I have committed neither of those, they do not apply, at least in my case.'

She flinched again, and Antonios registered her reaction with a curl of his lip. 'Why do you want me to return to Greece, Antonios?'

'Not, as you seem to fear, to resume our marriage.' His voice hardened as he raked her with a contemptuous gaze. 'I have no desire to do that.'

Of course he didn't. And that shouldn't hurt, because she'd chosen it to be that way, and yet it still did. 'Then…'

'My mother, as you might remember, was fond of you. She doesn't know why you left, and I have not enlightened her as to the state of our marriage.'

Guilt twisted sharply inside her. Daphne Marakaios had been kind to her during her time in Greece, but it still hadn't been enough to stay. To stay sane.

'Why haven't you told her?' Lindsay asked. 'It's been six months already, and you can't keep it a secret forever.'

'Why shouldn't you tell her?' Antonios countered. 'Oh, I forgot. Because you're a coward. You sneak away from my home and my bed and can't even be bothered to have a single conversation about why you wished to end our marriage.'

Lindsay drew a deep breath, fighting the impulse to tell him just how many conversations she'd tried to have. There was no point now. 'I understand that you're angry—'

'I'm not angry, Lindsay. To be angry I would have to care.' He stood up, the expression on his face ironing out. 'And I stopped caring when you sent me that email. When you refused to say anything but that our marriage was a mistake when I called you, wanting to know what had happened. When you showed me how little you thought of me or our marriage.'

'And you showed me how little you thought of our marriage every day I was in Greece,' Lindsay returned before she could help herself.

Antonios turned to her slowly, his eyes wide with incredulity. 'Are you actually going to blame me for the end of our marriage?' he asked, each syllable iced with disbelief.

'Oh, no, of course not,' Lindsay fired back. 'How could I do that? How could you possibly have any responsibility or blame?'

He stared at her, his eyes narrowing, and Lindsay almost laughed to realize he wasn't sure if she was being sarcastic or not.

Then he shrugged her words aside and answered in a clipped voice, 'I *don't* care, about you or your reasons. But my mother does. Because she has been ill, I have spared her the further grief of knowing how and why you have gone.'

'Ill—'

'Her cancer has returned,' Antonios informed her with brutal bluntness. 'She got the results back a month after you left.'

Lindsay stared at him in shock. She'd known Daphne had been in remission from breast cancer, but the outlook had been good. 'Antonios, I'm so sorry. Is it…is it treatable?'

He lifted one powerful shoulder in a shrug, his expression veiled. 'Not very.'

Lindsay sank back in her chair, her mind reeling with this new information. She thought of kind Daphne, with her white hair and soft voice, her gentleness apparent in every word and action, and felt a twist of grief for the woman she'd known so briefly. And as for Antonios… he adored his mother. This would have hit him hard and she, his wife, hadn't been there to comfort and support him through her illness. Yet would she have been able to, if she'd stayed in Greece?

She'd been so desperately unhappy there, and the thought of returning brought the old fears to the fore.

'Antonios,' she said quietly, 'I'm very, very sorry about your mother, but I still can't go back to Greece.'

'You can and you will,' Antonios replied flatly, 'if you want a divorce.'

She shook her head, her hair flying, desperation digging its claws into her soul. 'Then I won't ask for a divorce.'

'Then you are my wife still, and you belong with me.' His voice had roughened and he turned away from her in one sharp movement. 'You cannot have it both ways, Lindsay.'

'How will my seeing your mother help her?' Lindsay protested. 'It would only hurt her more for me to tell her to her face that we've separated—'

'But I have no intention of having you tell her that.' Antonios turned around, his eyes seeming to burn right through her as he glared at her. 'It is likely my mother only has a few months to live, perhaps less. I do not intend to distress her with the news of our failed marriage. For a few days, Lindsay, perhaps a week, you can pretend that we are still happily married.'

'What—?' She stared at him, appalled, as he gave her a grimace of a smile.

'Surely that is not impossible? You have already proven once what a good actress you are, when you pretended to fall in love with me.'

Antonios stared at his wife's lovely pale face and squashed the tiny flicker of pity he felt for her. She looked so trapped, so *horrified* at the prospect of resuming their marriage and returning to Greece.

Not, of course, that they would truly resume

their marriage. It would be a sham only, for the sake of his mother. Antonios had no intention of inviting Lindsay into his bed again. Not after she'd left him in such a cold-hearted and cowardly way. No, he'd take her back to Greece for a few days for his mother's sake, and then he'd never see her again…which was what she obviously wanted. And he wanted it, too.

'A few days?' she repeated numbly. 'And that will be enough…'

'It's my mother's name day next week,' Antonios told her.

'Name day…'

'In Greece we celebrate name days rather than birthdays. My family wishes to celebrate it especially, considering.' Grief constricted his throat and burned in his chest. He could not imagine Villa Marakaios without his mother. Losing his father had been hard enough. His father had built the vineyard from nothing; he'd been the brains behind the operation, for better and definitely for worse, but his mother had always been its heart. And when the heart was gone…

But perhaps his own heart had already gone, crushed to nothing when his wife had left him.

He'd thought Lindsay had loved him. He'd believed they were happy together.

What a joke. What a lie. But Antonios knew he should be used to people not being what they seemed. Not saying what they meant. He'd had hard lessons in that already.

'We are having a celebration,' he continued, just managing to keep his voice even. 'Family and friends, all our neighbours. You will be there. Afterwards you can return here if you wish. I will explain to my mother that you needed to finish your research.' He knew Lindsay had been pursuing her doctorate in Pure Mathematics, and when she'd left him she'd told him she needed to tie a few things up back in New York. He'd said goodbye in good faith, thinking she'd only be gone a few days. She'd already told him that her research could be done anywhere; she'd said there was nothing for her back in New York. But apparently that, like everything else, had been a lie.

Lindsay's face had gone even paler and she lifted one hand to her throat, swallowing convulsively. 'A party? Antonios, please. I can't.'

Fury beat through his blood. 'What did I ever do to you,' he demanded in a low, savage voice, 'to make you treat me this way? Treat my family this way? We welcomed you into our home, into our lives.' His insides twisted as emotion gripped him—emotion he couldn't bear Lindsay to see. He'd told her he didn't care about her any more, and he'd meant it. He had to mean it. 'My mother,' he said after a moment, when he'd regained his composure and his voice was as flat and toneless as he needed it to be, 'loved you. She treated you like her own daughter. Is this how you intend to repay her?'

Tears sparkled on Lindsay's lashes and she blinked them back, shaking her head in such obvious misery that Antonios almost felt sorry for her again. Almost.

'No, of course not,' she said in a low voice. 'I…I was very grateful to your mother, and her kindness to me.'

'You have a funny way of showing it.'

Her eyes flashed fire at that, and Antonios wondered what on earth she had to be angry about. *She'd* left *him*.

'Even so,' she said quietly, one hand still fluttering at her throat, 'it is very difficult for me to return to Greece.'

'And why is that? Do you have a lover waiting for you here in New York?'

Her mouth dropped open in shock. 'A lover—'

Antonios shrugged, as if it were a matter of no consequence, even though the thought of Lindsay with another man, violating their marriage vows, their marriage *bed*, made him want to punch something. 'I do not know what else would take you so abruptly from Greece.' *From me*, he almost said, but thankfully didn't.

She shook her head slowly, her eyes wide, although with what emotion Antonios couldn't tell. 'No,' she said in a low voice. 'I don't have a lover. There's only been you, Antonios. Ever.'

And yet he obviously hadn't been enough. Antonios didn't even know whether to believe her; he told himself it didn't matter. 'Then there is no reason for you not to come to Greece.'

'My research—'

'Cannot wait a week?' Impatience flared inside him, along with the familiar fury. Didn't she realize how thoughtless, how selfish and cruel she was being?

Even now, after six months of coming to accept and learning to live with her abandonment, he was stunned by how completely she'd deceived him. He had believed in her love for him utterly. But, Antonios reminded himself, they'd only known each other a week when they had married. It had been impulsive, reckless even, but he'd been so *sure*. Sure of his love for Lindsay, and of her love for him.

What a fool he'd been.

Lindsay was staring at him, her face still pale and miserable. 'One week,' Antonios ground out. 'Seven days. And then I intend never to see you again.' She flinched, as if his words hurt her, and he let out a hard laugh. 'Doesn't that notion please you?'

She glanced away, pressing her lips together to keep them from trembling. 'No,' she said after a moment. 'It doesn't.'

He shook his head slowly. 'I don't understand you.'

'I know.' She let out a shuddering breath. 'You never did.'

'And that is my fault?'

She shook her head wearily. 'It's too late to apportion blame, Antonios. It simply is. Was. Our marriage was a mistake, as I told you in my email and on the telephone.'

'Yet you never said why.'

'You never asked,' Lindsay answered, her voice sharpening, and Antonios frowned at her.

'I asked you on the phone—'

'No,' Lindsay told him quietly, 'you didn't. You asked me if I were serious, and I said yes. And then you hung up.'

Antonios stared at her, his jaw bunched so tight it ached. 'You're the one who left, Lindsay.'

'I know—'

'Yet now you are attempting to imply that our marriage failed because I didn't ask the right questions when I called you after you'd left me. *Theos!* It is hard to take.'

'I'm not implying anything of the sort, Antonios. I was simply reminding you of the facts.'

'Then let me remind you of a fact. I'm not interested in your explanations. The time for those has passed. What I am interested in, Lindsay—

the *only* thing I am interested in—is your agreement. A plane leaves for Athens tonight. If we are to be on it, we need to leave here in the next hour.'

'What?' Her gaze flew back to his, her mouth gaping open. 'I haven't even agreed.'

'Don't you want a divorce?'

She stared at him for a moment, her chin lifted proudly, her eyes cool and grey. 'You might think you can blackmail me into agreeing, Antonios,' she told him, 'but you can't. I'll come to Greece, not because I want a divorce but because I want to pay my respects to your mother. To explain to her—'

'Do not think—' Antonios cut her off '—that you'll tell her some sob story about our mistake of a marriage. I don't want her upset—'

'When do you intend on telling her the truth?'

'Never,' Antonios answered shortly. 'She doesn't have that long to live.'

Tears filled Lindsay's eyes again, turning them luminous and silver, and she blinked them back. 'Do you really think that's the better course? To deceive her—'

'You're one to speak of deception.'

'I never deceived you, Antonios. I did love you, for that week in New York.'

The pain that slashed through him was so intense and sudden that Antonios nearly gasped aloud. Nearly clutched his chest, as if he were having a heart attack, the same as his father, dead at just fifty-nine years old. 'And then?' he finally managed, his voice thankfully dispassionate. 'You just stopped?' Part of him knew he shouldn't be asking these questions, shouldn't care about these answers. He'd told Lindsay the time for explanations had passed, and it had. 'Never mind,' he dismissed roughly. 'It hardly matters. Come to Greece for whatever reason you want, but you need to be ready in an hour.'

She stared at him for a long moment, looking fragile and beautiful and making him remember how it had felt to hold her. Touch her.

'Fine,' she said softly, and her voice sounded sad and resigned. Suppressing the ache of longing that trembled through him, Antonios turned away from the sight of his wife and waited, his hands clenched into fists at his sides, as she packed up her belongings and then, without a word or glance for him, slipped by him and out of the room.

CHAPTER TWO

LINDSAY WALKED ACROSS the college campus in the oncoming twilight with Antonios like a malevolent shadow behind her. She walked blindly, unaware of the stately brick buildings, now gilded in the gold of fading sunlight, that made this small liberal arts college one of the most beautiful in the whole north-east of America.

All she could think of was the week that loomed so terribly ahead of her. All she could feel was Antonios's anger and scorn.

Maybe she deserved some of it, leaving the way she had, but Antonios had no idea how hard life in Greece had been for her. Hadn't been willing to listen to her explanations, fumbling and faltering as they had been, because while she'd wanted him to understand she'd also been afraid of him knowing and seeing too much.

Their marriage, Lindsay acknowledged hollowly, had been doomed from the start, never mind that one magical week in New York.

And now the time for explanations had passed, Antonios said. It was for the best, Lindsay knew, because having Antonios understand her or her reasons for leaving served no purpose now. It was impossible anyway, because he'd *never* understood. Never tried.

'Where do you live?' Antonios asked as they passed several academic buildings. A few students relaxed outside, lounging in the last of the weak October sunshine before darkness fell. Fall had only just come to upstate New York; the leaves were just starting to change and the breeze was chilly, but after a long, sticky summer of heatwaves everyone was ready for autumn.

'Just across the street,' Lindsay murmured. She crossed the street to a lane of faculty houses, made of clapboard and painted in different bright colours with front porches that held a few Adonirack chairs or a porch swing. She'd sat outside there, in the summers, watching the world go by. Always a spectator…until she'd met Antonios.

He'd woken her up, brought her into the land of the living. With him she'd felt more joy and excitement than she'd ever known before. She should have realized it couldn't last, it hadn't been real.

Antonios stood patiently while she fumbled for the keys; to her annoyance and shame her hands shook. He affected her that much. And not just him, but the whole reality he'd thrust so suddenly upon her. Going to Greece. Seeing his family again. Pretending to be his wife—his *loving* wife—again. Parties and dinners, endless social occasions, every moment in the spotlight…

'Let me help you,' Antonios said and, to her surprise, he almost sounded gentle. He took the key from her hand and fitted it into the lock, turning it easily before pushing the door open.

Lindsay muttered her thanks and stepped inside, breathed in the musty, dusty scent of her father's house. It was strange to have Antonios here, to see this glimpse of her old life, the only life she'd known until he had burst into it.

She flipped on the light and watched him blink as he took in the narrow hallway, made even narrower by the bookshelves set against every wall, each one crammed to overflowing with books. More books were piled on the floor in teetering stacks; the dining room table was covered in textbooks and piles of papers. Lindsay was so used to it that she didn't even notice the clutter any more, but she was conscious of it now, with Antonios here. She was uncomfortably aware of just how small and messy it all was. Yet it was also home, the place where she'd felt safe, where she and her father had been happy, or as happy as they knew how to be. She wouldn't apologize for it.

She cleared her throat and turned towards the stairs. 'I'll just pack.'

'Do you need any help?'

She turned back to Antonios, surprised by his solicitude. Or was he being patronizing? She couldn't tell anything about him any more; his expression was veiled, his voice toneless, his movements controlled.

'No,' she answered, 'I'm fine.'

He arched one dark eyebrow. 'Are you really fine, Lindsay? Because just now your hands were shaking too much for you even to open your front door.'

She stiffened, colour rushing into her face. 'Maybe that's because you're so angry, Antonios. It's a little unsettling to be around someone like that.'

His mouth tightened. 'You think I shouldn't be angry?'

She closed her eyes briefly as weariness swept over her. 'I don't want to get into this discussion. We've both agreed it serves no purpose. I was just—'

'Stating a fact,' Antonios finished sardonically. 'Of course. I'm sorry I can't make this experience easier for you.'

Lindsay just shook her head, too tired and tense to argue. 'Please, let's not bicker and snipe at each other. I'm coming to Greece as you wanted. Can't that be enough?'

His eyes blazed and he took a step towards her, colour slashing his cheekbones. 'No, Lindsay, that is not remotely enough. But since it is all I have asked of you, and all I believe you are capable of, I will have to be satisfied.'

He stared at her for a long, taut moment; Lindsay could hear her breathing turn ragged as her heart beat harder. She felt trapped by his gaze, pinned as much by his contempt as her own pointless anger. And underneath the fury that simmered in Antonios's gaze and hid in her own heart was the memory of when things had been different between them. When he'd taken her in his arms and made her body sing. When she'd thought she loved him.

Then he flicked his gaze away and, sagging with relief, she turned and went upstairs.

She dragged a suitcase out of the hall closet, forced herself to breathe more slowly. She could do this. She *had* to do this, not because she wanted a divorce so badly but because she owed it to Daphne. Her own mother had turned her back on her completely when she'd been no more than a child, and Daphne's small kindnesses to her had been like water in a barren desert. But not enough water. Just a few drops dribbled on her parched lips, when she'd needed the oasis of her husband's support and understanding, attention and care.

'Lindsay?' She heard the creak of the staircase as Antonios came upstairs, his broad shoulders nearly touching both walls as he loomed in the hallway, tall and dark, familiar and strange at the same time. 'We need to leave shortly.'

'I'll try to hurry.' She started throwing clothes into her suitcase, dimly aware that she had nothing appropriate for the kind of social occasions Antonios would expect her to attend. Formal dinners, a huge party for Daphne…as the largest local landowner and businessman, Antonios's calendar had been full of social engagements. From the moment she'd arrived in Greece he'd expected her to be his hostess, to arrange seating for dinner parties, to chat effortlessly to everyone, to be charming and sparkling and always at his side, except when he'd left her for weeks on end to go on business trips. Lindsay didn't know which had been worse: trying to manage alone or feeling ignored.

In any case, she hadn't managed, not remotely.

Being Antonios's wife was a role she had been utterly unprepared for.

And now she'd have to go through it all again, all the social occasions and organizing, and, worse, it would be under his family's suspicious gaze because she'd been gone for so long. Her breath hitched at the thought.

Don't think about it. You can deal with that later. Just focus on the present.

The present, Lindsay acknowledged, was difficult enough.

'You left plenty of clothes at the villa,' Antonios told her. 'You only need to pack a small amount.'

Lindsay pictured all the clothes back in their bedroom, the beautiful things Antonios had bought her in New York, before he'd taken her back to Greece. She'd forgotten about them, and the thought of them waiting for her there, hanging in the closet as if she'd never left, made her feel slightly sick.

'I'll just get my toiletries,' she said, and turned to go to the bathroom down the hall. She had to move past him in the narrow hallway and, as she tried to slip past his powerful form, she could smell his aftershave and feel the press of his back against her breasts. For one heart-stopping second she longed to throw herself into his arms, wrap herself around him, feel the comforting heat of his body, the sensuous slide of his lips on hers. To feel wanted and cherished and safe again.

It was never going to happen.

Antonios moved to let her pass and her breath came out in a shuddering rush as she quickly slipped towards the bathroom and, caught between relief and despair, shut and locked the door.

Ten minutes later she'd packed one small case and Antonios brought it down to the hired car he had waiting in one of the college car parks. Lindsay slipped into the leather interior, laid her head back against the seat. She felt incredibly, unbearably tired.

'Do you need to notify anyone?' Antonios asked. 'That you're leaving?'

'No.' Her research, as he'd so bluntly pointed out, could wait. She'd stopped her work as a teaching assistant for introductory classes after her father had died last summer. Only nine months ago, and yet it felt like a lifetime.

It *had* been a lifetime.

'No one will worry about you?' Antonios asked. 'Or wonder where you've gone?'

'I'll email my colleagues. They'll understand.'

'Did you tell them about me?'

'You know I did,' she answered. 'I had to explain why I left my job and house and went to Greece on the spur of the moment.'

His hands flexed on the steering wheel; she could feel his tension. 'It was your choice, Lindsay.'

'I know it was.'

'You said you had nothing left back in New York.'

'It felt like I didn't.'

He shifted in his seat, seeming to want to say more, but kept himself from it.

Lindsay turned her face to the window, steeled herself for the next endless week of tension like this, stalled conversations and not-so-veiled hostility. How on earth were they going to convince

Daphne, as well as the rest of his family, that they were still in love?

They didn't speak for the rest of the three-hour drive to New York City. Antonios returned the rental car and took their suitcases into the airport; within a few minutes after checking in they'd been whisked to a first-class lounge and treated to champagne and canapés.

It seemed ludicrous to be sitting in luxury and sipping champagne as if they were on honeymoon. As if they were in love.

Lindsay sneaked a glance at Antonios—the dark slashes of his eyebrows drawn together, his mouth turned downwards in a forbidding frown—and she had a sudden, absurd urge to say something silly, to make him smile.

The truth was, she didn't know what she felt for him any more. Sadness for what she'd thought they had, and anger for the way he'd shown her it was false. Yet she'd been so in love with him during their time in New York. It was hard to dismiss those feelings as mere fantasy, and yet she knew she had to.

And in a few hours she'd have to pretend they

were real, that she still felt them. Her breath hitched at the thought.

'Does anyone know?' she asked and Antonios snapped his gaze to hers.

'Know what?'

'That we're…that we're separated.'

His mouth thinned. 'We're not, in actuality, legally separated, but no, no one knows.'

'Not any of your sisters?' she pressed. She thought of his three sisters: bossy Parthenope, with a husband and young son, social butterfly Xanthe, and Ava, her own age yet utterly different from her. She hadn't bonded with any of them during her time in Greece; his sisters had been possessive of Antonios, and had regarded his unexpected American bride with wary suspicion. They'd also, at Antonios's command, backed off from all the social responsibilities they'd fulfilled for him when he'd been a bachelor. A sign of respect, Antonios had told her, but Lindsay had seen the disdain in their covert glances. What they'd done so effortlessly, maintaining and even organizing the endless social whirl, had been nearly impossible for her. They'd realized that, even if Antonios hadn't.

And now she would have to face them again, suffer them giving her guarded looks, asking her questions, demanding answers…

She couldn't do this.

'Is the thought of my family so abhorrent to you?' Antonios demanded, and Lindsay stiffened.

'No—'

'Because,' he told her bluntly, 'you look like you're going to be sick.'

'I'm not going to be sick.' She took a deep breath. 'But the thought of seeing your family again does make me nervous, Antonios—'

'They did nothing but welcome you.' He cut her off with a shrug of his powerful shoulders.

She took a measured breath. 'Only at your command.'

He arched an eyebrow. 'Does that matter?'

Of course it does. She bit back the words, knowing they would only lead to pointless argument. 'I don't think they were pleased that you came home with such an unexpected bride,' she said after a moment. 'I think they would have preferred you to marry someone of your own background.' A good Greek wife…the kind of wife she hadn't, and never could have, been.

'Perhaps,' Antonios allowed, his tone still dismissive, 'but they still accepted you because they knew I loved you.'

Lindsay didn't answer. It was clear Antonios hadn't seen how suspicious his sisters had been of her. And while they *had* accepted her on the surface, there had still been plenty of sideways glances, speculative looks, even a few veiled comments. Lindsay had felt every single one, to the core.

Yet she wasn't about to explain that to Antonios now, not when he looked so fierce—fiercely determined to be in the right.

'You have nothing to say to that?' Antonios asked, and Lindsay shrugged, taking a sip of champagne. It tasted sour in her mouth.

'No, I don't.' Nothing he would be willing to hear, anyway.

His mouth tightened and he turned to stare out of the floor-to-ceiling windows overlooking the runway. Lindsay watched him covertly, despair and longing coursing through her in equal measures.

She told herself she shouldn't feel this much emotion. It had been her choice to leave, and really they'd known so little of each other. Three months together, that was all. Not enough time to fall in love, much less stay there.

She was a mathematician; she believed in reason, in fact, in logic. Love at almost first sight didn't figure in her world view. Her research had shown the almost mystical relationships between numbers, but she and Antonios weren't numbers, and even though her heart had once cried out differently her head insisted they couldn't have actually loved each other.

'Maybe you never really loved me, Antonios,' she said quietly, and he jerked back in both shock and affront.

'Is that why you left? Because you didn't think I loved you?' he asked in disbelief.

'I'm trying to explain how I felt,' Lindsay answered evenly. 'Since you seem determined to draw an explanation from me, even if you say you don't want one.'

'So you've convinced yourself I didn't love you.' He folded his arms, his face settling into implacable lines.

'I don't think either of us had enough time to truly love or even know each other,' Lindsay answered. 'We only knew each other a week—'

'Three months, Lindsay.'

'A week before we married,' she amended. 'And it was a week out of time, out of reality…' Which was what had made it so sweet and so precious. A week away from the little life she'd made for herself in New York—a life that had been both prison and haven. A week away from being Lindsay Douglas, brilliant mathematician and complete recluse. A week of being seen in an entirely new way—as someone who was interesting and beautiful and *normal*.

'It may have only been a week,' Antonios said, 'but I knew you. At least, I thought I knew you. But perhaps you are right, because the woman I thought I knew wouldn't have left me the way you did.'

'Then you didn't really know me,' Lindsay answered, and Antonios swung round to stare at her, his eyes narrowed.

'Is there something you're not telling me?'

'I…' She drew a deep breath. She could tell him now, explain everything, yet what good would it do? Their marriage was over. Her leaving him had brought about its end. But before she could even think about summoning the courage to confess, he had turned away from her again.

'It doesn't matter,' he answered. 'I don't care.'

Lindsay sagged back against her seat, relief and disappointment flooding her as she told herself it was better this way. It had to be.

Antonios sat in his first-class seat, his glass of complimentary champagne untouched, as his mind seethed with questions he'd never thought to ask himself before. And he shouldn't, he knew, ask them now. It didn't matter what Lindsay's reasons had been for leaving, or whether they'd truly known and loved each other or not.

Any possibility between them had ended with her two-sentence email.

Dear Antonios,
I'm sorry, but I cannot come back to Greece. Our marriage was a mistake. Lindsay.

When he'd first read the email, he'd thought it was a joke. His brain simply hadn't been able to process what she was telling him; it had seemed so absurd. Only forty-eight hours before, he'd made love to her half the night long and she'd clung to him until morning, kissed him with passion and gentleness when she'd said goodbye.

And she'd known she was leaving him *then*?

He hadn't wanted to believe it, had started jumping to outrageous, nonsensical conclusions. Someone else had written the email. A jealous rival or a desperate relative? He'd cast them both in roles in a melodrama that had no basis in reality.

The reality was his phone call to Lindsay that same day, and her flat voice repeating what she'd told him in the email. Maybe he'd been the one to hang up, but only because she'd been so determined not to explain herself. Not to say anything at all, except for her wretched party line. That their marriage was a mistake.

Disbelief had given way to anger, to a cold, deep rage the like of which he'd never felt before, not even when he'd realized the extent of his father's desperate deception. He'd *loved* her. He'd brought her into the bosom of his family, showered her with clothes and jewels. He'd given her his absolute loyalty, had presented her to his shocked family as the choice of his heart, even though they'd only known each other for a week. He'd shown how devoted he was to her in every way possible, and she'd said it was all a *mistake*?

He turned to her now, took in her pale face, the soft, vulnerable curve of her cheek, a tendril of white-blonde hair resting against it. When he'd first seen her in New York City, he'd been utterly enchanted. She'd looked ethereal, like a winter fairy, with her pale hair and silvery eyes. He'd called her his Snow Queen.

'Did you intend to leave me permanently,' he asked suddenly, his voice too raw for his liking or comfort, 'when you said goodbye to me in

Greece?' When she'd kissed him, her slender arms wrapped around his neck, had she known?

She didn't turn from the window, but he felt her body tense. 'Does it matter?'

'It does to me.' Even though it shouldn't. But maybe he needed to ask these questions, despite what he'd said. Perhaps he would find some peace amidst all the devastation if he understood, even if only in part, why Lindsay had acted as she had. Perhaps then he could let go of his anger and hurt, and move on. Alone.

She let out a tiny sigh. 'Then, yes. I did.'

Her words were like a fist to his gut. To his heart. 'So you lied to me.'

'I never specified when I was coming back,' she said, her voice tired and sad.

'You never said you were going. You acted like you loved me.' He turned away from her, not wanting her to see the naked emotion he could feel on his face. She wasn't even looking at him, but he still felt exposed. Felt the raw pain underneath the anger. Still, one word squeezed its way out of his throat. 'Why?'

She didn't answer.

'Why, Lindsay?' he demanded. 'Why didn't you tell me you were planning to leave, that you were unhappy—?'

'I tried telling you the truth but you never heard it,' she said wearily. 'You never listened.'

'What are you talking about?' Antonios demanded. 'You never once said you were unhappy—'

Lindsay shook her head. 'I don't want to go into it, Antonios. It's pointless. If you want an explanation, it's this: I never really loved you.'

He blinked, reeling from the coldly stated fact even as he sought to deny it. 'Why did you marry me, then?' he asked when he trusted his voice to sound even. Emotionless.

'Because I thought I loved you. I convinced myself what we had was real.' She turned to him, her eyes blazing with what he realized, to his own shock, was anger or maybe grief. 'Can't you see how it was for me? My father had died only a few weeks before. I went to New York because I wanted to escape my life, escape my loneliness and grief. I wandered around the city like a lost soul, still feeling so desperately sad and yet wanting to be enchanted by all the beauty. And then you saw me and you told me *you* were lost, and when I looked in your eyes it felt like you were seeing me—a me I hadn't even known existed until that moment.'

She sank back against her seat, out of breath, her face pale, her shoulders rising and falling in agitation. Antonios's mind spun emptily for a few stunned seconds before he finally managed, his voice hoarse, 'And that was real.'

'No, it wasn't, Antonios. It was a fairy tale. It was playing at being in love. It was red roses and dancing until midnight and penthouse suites at luxury hotels. It was wonderful and magical, but it wasn't *real*.'

'Just because something is exciting—'

'Real was coming to Greece—' she cut across him flatly '—and discovering what your life was like there. Real was feeling like I was drowning every day and you never even noticed.' She bit her lip and then turned towards the window; he realized she'd turned to hide her own emotion, just as he'd tried to hide his. The anger that had been a cold, hard ball inside him started to soften, but he didn't know what emotion replaced it. He felt confused and unsteady, as if someone had given him a hard push, had scattered all his tightly held beliefs and resolutions.

'Lindsay…' He put a hand on her shoulder, conscious once again of how small and fragile she seemed. 'I don't understand.'

She let out a choked laugh and dashed quickly at her eyes. 'I know, Antonios, and you never did. But it's too late now, for both of us. You know that, so let's just stop this conversation.'

A stewardess came by to take their untouched champagne glasses and prepare them for take-off. Lindsay took the opportunity to shrug his hand from her shoulder and wipe the traces of tears from her eyes.

When she turned to look at him, her face was composed and carefully blank. 'Please, let's just get through this flight.'

He nodded tersely, knowing now was not the time to demand answers. And really, what answer could Lindsay give? What on earth could she mean, that she'd been drowning? He'd taken her to his home. His family had welcomed her.

He'd given her every comfort, every luxury. Just the memory of how she'd responded to his touch, how her body had sung in tune to his, made a bewildered fury rise up in him again. What the hell was she talking about—*drowning*?

And if she truly had been unhappy, why hadn't she ever told him?

CHAPTER THREE

AS SOON AS the sign for seat belts blinked off, Lindsay unbuckled hers and slipped past Antonios. She hurried to the first-class bathroom, barely taking in the spacious elegance, the crystal vase of roses by the sink. She placed her hands flat on the marble countertop and breathed slowly, in and out, several times, until her heart rate started to slow.

Telling him that much, confessing to even just a little of how she'd felt, had depleted every emotional resource she had. She had no idea how she was going to cope with seven more days of being with Antonios, of pretending to his family.

She pressed her forehead against the cool glass of the mirror and continued with her deep, even breathing. She couldn't panic now. Not like she had back in Greece, when the panic had taken over her senses, had left her feeling like an empty shell, a husk of a person, barely able to function.

How had Antonios not seen that? How had he not heard? Maybe her attempts at trying to explain had been feeble, but he hadn't wanted to listen. Hadn't been able to hear. And he still couldn't.

She'd refuse to discuss it any more, Lindsay resolved. She couldn't defuse his anger and she wouldn't even try. Survival was all she was looking for now, for the next week. For Daphne's sake. Her mother-in-law deserved that much, and Lindsay wanted to see her again and pay her respects.

But heaven help her, it was going to be hard.

Taking a deep breath, she splashed some water on her face and patted it dry. With one last determined look at her pale face in the mirror, she turned and headed back to their seats.

Their dinners had arrived while Lindsay was in the bathroom, and she gazed at the linen napkins and tablecloth, the crystal wine glasses and the silver-domed chafing dishes, remembering how they'd travelled like this to Greece. How luxurious and decadent she'd felt, lounging with Antonios as they ate, heads bent together, murmuring and laughing, buoyant with happiness.

Utterly different from the silent tension that snapped between them now.

Antonios gestured to the dishes as she sat down. 'I didn't know what you wanted, so I ordered several things.'

'I'm sure it's all delicious.' And yet she had no appetite. Antonios lifted the lid on her meal and she stared at the beef, its rich red-wine sauce pooling on her plate, and twisted her napkin in her lap as her stomach rebelled at even the thought of eating.

'You are not hungry?' Antonios asked, one eyebrow arched, and Lindsay shook her head.

'No.'

'You should eat anyway. Keep up your strength.'

And God knew she needed what little she had. She picked up her fork and speared a piece of beef, putting it into her mouth and chewing mechanically. She couldn't taste anything.

Antonios noticed, one eyebrow lifting sardonically. 'Not good enough for you?' he queried, and she let out a little groan.

'Don't start, Antonios.'

'I can't help but wonder, when you had every luxury at your disposal, how you still managed to be so unhappy.'

'There is more to life than luxuries, Antonios. There's attention and support and care.' So much for her resolution not to talk about things.

'Are you saying I didn't give you those?' Antonios demanded.

'No, you didn't. Not the way I needed.'

'You never told me what you needed.'

'I tried,' she said wearily. She felt too tired to be angry any more, even though the old hurt still burrowed deep.

'When? When did you try?'

'Time and time again. I told you I was uncomfortable at all the parties, never mind playing hostess—'

His brow wrinkled and Lindsay knew he probably didn't even remember the conversations she'd found so difficult and painful. 'I told you it would get better in time,' he finally answered. 'That you just needed to let people get to know you.'

'And I told you that was hard for me.'

He shrugged her words aside, just as he had every time she'd tried to tell him before. 'That's not a reason to leave a marriage, Lindsay.'

'Maybe not for you.'

'Are you actually saying you left me simply because you didn't like going to parties?'

'No.' She took a deep breath. 'I left you because you never listened to me. Because you dumped me in Greece like another suitcase you'd acquired and never paid any attention to me again.'

'I had to work, Lindsay.'

'I know that. Trust me, Antonios, I know that. You worked all the time.'

'You never acted like it bothered you—'

She let out a laugh, high and shrill, the sound surprising them both. 'You never change, do you? I'm trying to tell you how I felt and you just keep insisting I couldn't have felt that way, that you never knew. This is why I left, Antonios.' She gestured to the space between them.

'Because the way we were together in real life, not in some fairy-tale bubble in New York, didn't work. It made me miserable—more miserable than I'd ever been before—and that's saying something.'

He frowned. 'What do you mean, that's saying something?'

'Never mind.' She'd never told him about her mother, and never would. Some things were better left unsaid, best forgotten. Not that she could ever forget the way her mother had left.

This isn't what I expected.

A hot lump of misery formed in Lindsay's throat and she swallowed hard, trying to dislodge it. She didn't want to cry, not on an aeroplane, not in front of Antonios.

'*Theos*, Lindsay, if you're not going to tell me things, how can I ever understand you?'

'I don't want you to understand me, Antonios,' she answered thickly. 'Not any more. All I want is a divorce. And I assume you want that, too.' She took a shaky breath. 'Do you really want to be with a wife who left you, who doesn't love you?'

Fire flashed in his eyes and she knew it had been a low and cruel blow. But if that was what it took to get Antonios to stop with his questions, then so be it.

He leaned forward, his eyes still flashing, his mouth compressed. 'Do I need to remind you of how much you loved me, Lindsay? Every night in New York. Every night we were together in Greece.'

And, despite her misery, desire still scorched through her at the memory. 'I'm not talking about in bed, Antonios.'

'Because you certainly responded to me there. Even when you were supposedly *drowning*.'

She closed her eyes, tried to fight the need his simply stated words caused to well up inside her. Sex had always been good between them, had been a respite from the misery she'd faced every day. Maybe that made her weak or wanton, to have craved a man who'd hurt her heart, but she had. From the moment they'd met, she had. And some treacherous part of her still craved him now.

She felt Antonios's hand on her knee and her eyes flew open. 'What—?'

'It didn't take much to make you melt,' he said softly, the words as caressing as his hand. His hand slid up her thigh, his fingers sure and seeking. Lindsay froze, trapped by his knowing gaze and his even more knowing hand. 'I knew just where to touch you, Lindsay. Just how to make you scream. You screamed my name, do you remember?'

Heat flooded through her and she had to fight to keep from responding to his caress. 'Don't,' she whispered, but even to her own ears her voice sounded feeble.

'Don't what?' he asked, his voice so soft and yet also menacing. 'Don't touch you?' He slid his hand higher, cupping her between her legs. Just the press of his hand through her jeans made her stifle a moan as desire pulsed insistently through her.

'What are you trying to prove, Antonios?' she forced out, willing her body to stay still and not respond to his caress. 'That I desire you? Fine. I do. I always did. It doesn't change anything.'

'It should,' Antonios said, and he popped the button on her jeans, slid his hand down so his fingers brushed between her thighs, the sensation of his skin against hers so exquisite she gasped aloud, her eyes fluttering closed. Couldn't keep her hips from lifting off the seat.

Lindsay pressed her head back against the seat, memories and feelings crashing through her. He always had known just how to touch her, to please her. He still did, but there was no love or even kindness behind his calculated caresses now. With what felt like superhuman effort she opened her eyes, stared straight into his triumphant face, and said the thing that she knew would hurt him most.

'You might make me come, Antonios, but you can't make me love you.'

He stared back at her, his expression freezing, and then in one deft movement he yanked his hand from her, unbuckled his seat belt and disappeared through the curtains.

Lindsay sagged back against her seat, her jeans still undone, her heart thudding, and swallowed a sob.

* * *

Antonios strode down the first-class aisle, feeling trapped and angry and even dirty. He shouldn't have treated Lindsay like that. Shouldn't have used her desire, her body against her.

Shouldn't have been that pathetic.

What had he been trying to prove? That she felt something for him? He stood in the alcove that separated the first class from business and stared out into the endless night. He didn't know what he'd been trying to do. He'd just been acting, or perhaps reacting, to Lindsay's assertion that she didn't love him. That their love hadn't been real.

It had sure as hell felt real to him. But he'd told her he didn't love her any more, and he needed that to be true. He'd made sure it was true for the last six months, even as he'd maintained the odious front to his family that their marriage was still going strong. He'd had to, for his mother's sake as well as his own pride.

Or maybe you were just actually hoping she'd come back. Fool that you are, you still wanted her back. Because you loved her. Because you made promises.

And was that what was driving him now? The desire, the need to have Lindsay back in his life? Back as his wife? Or was it an even more shameful reason, one born of revenge and pride? Did he want to make her hurt the way he had, to pay for the way she'd treated him?

Antonios had no answer but he was resolved to stop this pointless back and forth, demanding answers that he knew would never satisfy him. The reasons she'd given him for leaving their marriage had been ridiculous. Maybe he had been working too hard, maybe he'd even ignored her a little, but that didn't mean you just walked out.

Except to Lindsay it seemed it did, and nothing, no revenge or explanation, could change that cold fact. His mouth a grim line of resolution, Antonios headed back to their seats.

Lindsay had tidied herself in his absence, her jeans buttoned back up, her face turned towards the window. She didn't move as he slid into the seat next to her. Didn't even blink.

'I'm sorry,' Antonios said in a low voice. 'I shouldn't have done that.' Lindsay didn't answer, didn't acknowledge his words in any way. 'Lindsay…'

'Just leave me alone, Antonios,' she said, and to his shame her voice sounded quiet and sad. Broken. 'It's going to be hard enough pretending we're still in love for your family. Don't make it any harder.'

He watched her for a moment, part of him aching to reach out and tuck her hair behind her ear, trail his fingers along the smoothness of her cheek. Comfort her, when he'd been the cause of her pain and he knew she didn't want his comfort anyway.

'I'm going to sleep,' she said, and without looking at him she took off her shoes, reached for the eye mask. He watched as she reclined her seat and covered herself with a blanket, all with her face averted from him. Then she slid the eye mask down over her eyes and shut him out completely.

Lindsay lay rigid on her reclined seat, her eyes clenched shut under the mask as she tried to will herself to sleep and failed. She felt a seething mix of anger and regret, guilt and hurt. Her body still tingled from where Antonios had touched her. Her heart still ached.

Forget about it, she told herself yet again. *Just get through this week*. But how on earth was she going to get through this week, when being in Greece had been so hard even when Antonios had loved her, or thought he had, when she'd thought she'd loved him?

Now, with the anger and contempt she'd felt from Antonios, the hurt and frustration she felt herself…it was going to be impossible. Something had to change. To give.

She slipped off her eye mask, determined to confront him, only to find him gazing at her, the hard lines of his face softened by tenderness and despair, a look of such naked longing on his face that it stole her breath. She felt tears come to her eyes and everything in her ached with longing.

'Antonios…'

His face blanked immediately and his mouth compressed. 'Yes?'

'I…' What could she say? *Don't look at me like*

you hate me? Just then, he hadn't. Just then he'd looked at her as if he still loved her.

But he doesn't. He doesn't even know you, not the real you. And you don't love him. You can't.

'Nothing,' she finally whispered.

'Get some sleep,' Antonios said, and turned his head away. 'It's going to be a long day tomorrow.'

They arrived in Athens at eleven in the morning, the air warm and dry, the sky hard and bright blue, everything so different from the damp early fall of upstate New York. Being here again brought back memories in flashes of pain: the limo Antonios had had waiting outside the airport, filled with roses. The way he'd held and kissed her all the way to his villa in the mountains of central Greece, and how enchanted Lindsay had been, still carried away by the fairy tale.

It wasn't until the limo had turned up the sweeping drive framed by plane trees with the huge, imposing villa and all of the other buildings in the distance that she'd realized she'd been dealing in fantasies…and that she and Antonios would not be living alone in some romantic hideaway. His mother, his brother, Leonidas, his two unmarried sisters, an army of staff and employees—everyone lived at Villa Marakaios, which wasn't the sweet little villa with terracotta tiles and painted wooden shutters that Lindsay had naively been imagining. No, it was a complex, a hive of industry, a *city.* And when she'd stepped out of the limo into that bright, bright sunshine, every eye of every citizen of that city had been trained on her.

Her worst nightmare.

She'd seen everyone lined up in front of the villa—the family, the friends, the employees and house staff, everyone staring at her, a few people whispering and even pointing—and she'd forgotten how to breathe.

Antonios had propelled her forward, one hand on her elbow, and she'd gone, her vision already starting to tunnel as her chest constricted and the panic took over.

She hadn't felt panic like that since she'd been

a little girl, her mother's hand hard on her lower back, shoving her into a room full of academics.

Come on, Lindsay. Recite something for us.

Sometimes she'd managed to stumble through a poem her mother had made her memorize, and sometimes her brain had blanked and, with her mouth tightening in disappointment, her mother had dismissed her from the room.

After too many of those disappointments, she'd dismissed her from her life.

This isn't what I expected.

And, standing there in the glare of Greek sunshine, Lindsay had felt it all come rushing back. The panic. The shortness of breath. The horrible, horrible feeling of every eye on her, every person finding her wanting. And she'd blacked out.

She'd come to consciousness inside the house, lying on a sofa, a cool cloth pressed to her head and a white-haired woman smiling kindly down at her.

'It's the sun, I'm sure,' Daphne Marakaios had said as she'd pressed the cloth to Lindsay's head. 'It's so strong here in the mountains.'

'Yes,' Lindsay had whispered. 'The sun.'

Now, as she slid into the passenger seat of Antonios's rugged SUV, having cleared customs and collected their luggage, she wondered if he even remembered how she'd fainted. He'd certainly been quick to accept it as her reaction to the sun, and she'd been too overwhelmed and shell-shocked to say any differently.

And she'd have to face his family again in just three hours. How on earth was she going to cope?

They drove out of Athens, inching through a mid-morning snarl of traffic, and then headed north on the National Highway towards Amfissa, the nearest town to Antonios's estate in the mountains.

With each mile they drove, Lindsay's panic increased. This time she knew what she was facing, and it would be so much worse. Now everyone would be suspicious, maybe even hostile. She could picture his sister Parthenope eyeing her with cool curiosity, her husband by her side and dark-haired, liquid-eyed little Timon clinging to her legs; Leonidas, Antonios's younger brother, giving her one of his sardonic looks;

Ava and Xanthe, his younger sisters, eyeing her with sceptical curiosity, as if they'd already decided she didn't belong. And the questions... she would have to answer so many questions...

'Antonios,' she said, his name little more than a croak, and he glanced at her briefly before snapping his gaze back to the road.

'What is it?'

She focused on her breathing, tried to keep it even. 'Would it...would it be possible for me to come to the villa quietly? I mean, not have everyone waiting and...I'd rather not see anyone at first.' *In. Out. In. Out.* With effort she kept her breathing measured and her heart rate started to slow. She could do this. She'd managed to control her anxiety for most of her life. She could do it now. She had to.

'The point,' Antonios returned, 'is for you to see people and be seen. No one thinks anything is wrong between us, Lindsay.'

But they would have guessed. Of course they would have guessed. His siblings weren't stupid, and neither was Daphne. Lindsay had been gone for six whole months and then Antonios had come all the way to New York to fetch her. Everyone would be wondering just what had gone wrong between them.

'I understand,' Lindsay said, her eyes closed as she pressed back against the seat and kept concentrating on those deep, even breaths. 'But I'd rather not have everyone there when we arrive.'

'What am I meant to do? Send them away?'

She opened her eyes as she tried to suppress a stab of irritation or even anger, wondering if he was deliberately being difficult. Or was he just obstinately obtuse, as usual? 'No, of course not. I just don't want them all lined up in front of the villa, waiting to welcome me.' Or not welcome, as the case well might be.

Antonios was silent for a moment, his gaze narrowed on the road in front of them, the sun glinting off the tarmac. 'You mean like last time.'

'Yes.'

'You fainted,' Antonios recalled slowly. 'When you got out of the car.'

So he had remembered. Just. 'Yes.'

Antonios's expression tightened and he turned

back to the road. 'I'll see what I can do,' he said, and they didn't speak for the rest of the journey.

Two hours later they'd left the highway for the narrow, twisting lane that curved its way between the mountains of Giona and Parnassus. They came around a bend and Villa Marakaios lay before them, nestled in a valley between the mountains, its many whitewashed buildings gleaming brightly under the afternoon sun.

Antonios drove down the twisting road towards the villa, his eyes narrowed against the sun, his mouth a hard, grim line.

As they drove through the gates he turned to the left, surprising her, for the front of the villa, with its many gleaming steps and impressive portico, was before them. Instead, Antonios drove around the back of the complex to a small whitewashed house with an enclosed courtyard and latticed shutters painted a cheerful blue. It looked, Lindsay thought in weary bemusement, like the villa she'd once imagined in her naive daydreams. A honeymoon house.

'We can stay here,' Antonios said tersely, and

he killed the engine. 'It's used as a guesthouse, but it's empty now.'

'What?' Lindsay stared at him in surprise. Last time they'd stayed in the main villa with all the family and staff; only Leonidas had his own place. Since his father's death, Antonios had been appointed the CEO of Marakaios Enterprises and essentially lord of the manor.

Now he shrugged and got out of the car. 'It will make it easier for us to maintain the pretence if we are not so much in the public eye.' He went around to the boot of the car for their cases, not looking at her as he added, 'And perhaps it will be easier for you.'

Lindsay stared at him, his dark head bent as he hefted their suitcases and then started walking towards the villa. He was being thoughtful, she realized. And he'd given credence to what she'd told him, if just a little.

'Thank you,' she murmured and with a wary, uncertain hope burgeoning inside her she followed him into the villa.

CHAPTER FOUR

ANTONIOS PUT THE suitcases in the villa's one bedroom, tension knotting between his shoulders. Coming back to Villa Marakaios always gave him a sense of impending responsibility and pressure, the needs and concerns of the family and business descending on him like a shroud the moment he drove through the gates. But it was a shroud he wore willingly and a duty he accepted with pride, no matter what the cost.

He could hear Lindsay moving behind him, walking with the quiet grace and dignity she'd always possessed.

'Why don't you rest?' he said as he turned around. Lindsay stood in the doorway, her pale hair floating around her face in a silvery-golden cloud, her eyes wide and clear, yet also troubled. 'Everyone is coming for dinner tonight,' he continued. 'I need to see to some business. I'll come back before we have to leave. But I suppose you don't mind me working all hours now, do you?'

The less they saw each other, the better. Yet he still couldn't keep a feeling of bitterness or maybe even hurt from needling him when she nodded, and wordlessly he walked past her and out of the villa.

He walked across the property to the offices housed separately from the family's living quarters, in a rambling whitewashed building overlooking the Marakaios groves that stretched to the horizon, rows upon rows of stately olive trees with their gnarled branches, each neatly pruned and tended, now just coming into flower.

He paused for a moment on the threshold of the building, steeling himself for the demands that would assail him the moment he walked in the door. Ten years after his father had told him of the extent of Marakaios Enterprises' debt, he'd finally brought the business to an even keel—but it had taken just about everything he had, both emotionally and physically.

Now he greeted his PA, Alysia, accepted a sheaf of correspondence and then strode into his office, perversely glad, for once, to immerse himself in paperwork and answering emails and not think of Lindsay.

Except he *did* think of Lindsay; she was like a ghost inside his mind, haunting his thoughts with both the good memories and the bad. The week in New York—that intense, incredible week when they'd shared everything.

And yet nothing, because he was realizing afresh just how much of a stranger she was.

In New York he'd thought he'd known her. She'd told him about her research, and he'd watched how animated she became when she talked about twin primes and Fermat's Last Theorem and Godel's proof for the existence of God. He hadn't really understood any of it, but he'd loved seeing her passion for her subject, intelligence and interest shining in her silver-grey eyes.

She'd told him about her father, too, who had died just a few weeks before they met. She'd cried then and he'd comforted her, drawing her into his arms, fitting her body around his as he'd tenderly wiped the tears from her face.

He thought about the first time they'd made love, how her eyes had gone so wide when he'd slid inside her and she'd said in wonder, 'It's like the most perfect equation,' which had made him laugh even as pleasure overtook them both. With Lindsay he'd felt happier than he ever had before. He'd felt *right*, complete in a way that made him realize just how much he'd been missing.

And then he recalled the emptiness that had swooped through him when he'd talked to her on the phone and she'd told him in that lifeless voice that it was all a mistake.

'Welcome back.'

Antonios looked up from his laptop to see his brother, Leonidas, lounging in the doorway of his office. Fourteen months younger, half an inch taller and a little leaner, Leonidas had been mistaken more than once for his twin. They'd been close as children, united in various boyish escapades, but since Antonios had become CEO the gulf between them had widened, and Antonios's vow of secrecy to his father made it impossible to bridge.

No one is to know, Antonios. No one but you. I couldn't bear it.

'Thank you,' he said now with a nod to Leonidas. He tried to offer his brother a smile, but the memories of Lindsay that had assailed him just now were still too poignant, too painful.

'Good trip?' Leonidas asked, one eyebrow cocked, and not for the first time Antonios wondered how much his brother knew, or at least guessed, about him and Lindsay.

'Fine,' he said briskly. 'Short. I thought about stopping in New York to see the new clients but there was no time.'

'I could do it,' Leonidas offered and Antonios shrugged.

'I'll travel back to New York next week, with Lindsay. I'll see them then.'

Leonidas's expression turned neutral as he gave a careless nod. 'So you're both returning to America in just one week?'

'Lindsay has research to finish.'

'I thought she could do it here.'

Antonios shrugged, hating the deception he was forced to maintain. First with his father, and now this. He'd accused Lindsay of lying to him, but he was the greater liar.

Soon, he told himself. Soon enough he would come clean. All too soon, when his mother was past knowing. The thought made him close his eyes briefly, and he snapped them open. 'She has to wrap up things with her house,' he said dismissively. 'You know how it is.'

Although of course Leonidas didn't know how it was. He was a determined bachelor and besides his private villa here he kept an apartment in Athens. Their father had appointed him as Head of European Operations before he'd died, and since then Leonidas had spent most of his time travelling to their various clients in Europe, working on new accounts because Antonios didn't want him to see the old ones. Couldn't let him know how close they'd come to losing it all.

'So she'll return when?' Leonidas asked and Antonios forced himself to shrug.

'We haven't decided on a date,' he answered coolly. 'Now, don't you have work to do? I just saw an email from the Lyon restaurant group. They're concerned about their supply.'

'I'm on it,' Leonidas answered, his voice terse, and he turned from the office.

Antonios sank back in his chair, raking his hands through his hair. Maintaining this deception was going to be even harder than he'd realized. And when he came clean…he burned to think of the disbelief and pity he'd face from his siblings.

Burned to think that it had come to this, and why? *Because Lindsay never loved you. And you didn't know her well enough to love her like you thought you did.*

Grimacing, he turned back to his laptop. He'd wasted enough time thinking about Lindsay today.

Lindsay managed to sleep for a couple of hours, waking muzzy-headed and disorientated to the sound of someone knocking on the door.

She stumbled out of bed, reaching for a robe hanging from the bathroom door to cover herself; it had been too warm to sleep in anything but her underwear. A maid whose face she vaguely recognized was standing outside, a man behind her carrying several suitcases.

'What…?' Lindsay began, confused and still only half awake.

'Kyrios Marakaios wanted your clothes to be brought here,' the maid explained in halting English. Lindsay knew only a few words of Greek. 'He asked for me to help put them away.'

'Oh…thank you.' She stepped back to let the woman in, and then watched uncomfortably as the man deposited the suitcases in the bedroom before leaving and the maid began unpacking the clothes she'd barely worn and then hanging them in the walk-in closet.

Lindsay offered to help but the woman insisted she'd do it herself, so she left the bedroom and went to the living area of the villa, gazing through the sliding glass doors that led to a private pool. If she were in the deep end of that thing, she thought disconsolately, she couldn't be more out of her depth.

Dinner, she knew, would be in just a few hours. She needed to get ready, and not just her clothes and make-up. She needed to prepare emotionally. Mentally.

Lindsay made herself some tea and took it outside to the pool area, sitting in one of the loungers and cradling the warmth of the mug between her hands as she closed her eyes and focused on her breathing. She pictured the ornate dining room where the family gathered for more formal meals, imagined each chair, each face, and focused on keeping her breathing slow and even.

Visualization, her therapist had told her, was meant to be helpful when trying to manage new or difficult situations. And she'd become good enough at it that she could picture it all and still stay calm.

It was when she was actually *in* the situation, facing all those people, all their stares and questions, that she started to panic.

'What are you doing?' Lindsay's eyes flew open and she saw Antonios standing by the gate that led out to the drive, his eyebrows drawn together in a frown. 'You sound like you're hyperventilating.'

'No, just breathing.' She felt a blush heat her cheeks and she took a sip of tea. 'Trying to relax.' And not succeeding very well.

Antonios's mouth twisted as he glanced around at the pool, the water sparkling in the bright sunlight, the whitewashed villa looking cool and pristine, everything beautiful and luxurious. Lindsay braced herself for some cutting remark about how difficult she must find it to relax in such a paradise. But to her relief he said nothing, just nodded towards the villa, his mouth tight.

'You should get dressed,' he said as he walked past her. 'We need to be at the main house in an hour.'

The maid had gone when Lindsay went back inside, and she spent a long time in the huge, sumptuous shower, as if she could postpone the inevitable moment when she faced Antonios's family.

He'd told her it was casual, which meant full make-up and a nice dress. The Marakaios family didn't do casual the way she'd ever understood it, and that just added to her stress and tension.

An hour later she stared at her reflection in

the bathroom mirror, wiped icy palms down the sides of the lavender linen shift that Antonios had bought for her in New York. She remembered the joy of trying on new clothes, parading them for him, laughing at his deliberately lascivious expressions. An ache of longing swept through her and she leaned her forehead against the mirror. They'd had so much fun together, for such a short while. No matter if it hadn't been real or lasting, she still missed that. Missed him, and missed the woman she'd been with him, before he'd taken her back to Greece. Before everything had gone wrong.

A sharp knock sounded on the bathroom door. 'Are you ready?' Antonios called. 'We need to go.'

'Okay.' Lindsay lifted her head from the mirror and stared at her reflection once more. Her heart was starting to beat fast, her chest to hurt, and she had that curious light-headed sensation that always preceded a full-blown panic attack.

Breathe, Lindsay. You can do this. You have to do this.

She gripped the edge of the sink, focused on her breathing and willed her heart rate to slow.

'Lindsay…' Antonios called, impatience edging his voice, and, after a few more agonized seconds of trying to keep the panic under control, she straightened and opened the door.

'I'm ready,' she said as she walked out of the bathroom. She was feeling light-headed enough to have to focus on her walking, the way a drunk person would. She didn't think she was very convincing because Antonios regarded her silently for a moment. She didn't look at him, just kept her chin held high, her shoulders back. *Breathe.*

'You look lovely,' Antonios said finally. 'I remember that dress.'

'Thank you.' It was hard to get words out of her throat, but she just about managed it. 'Why don't we go?'

She started out of the villa and Antonios followed. She stumbled slightly on the gravel drive and he took her arm, exclaiming as he did so.

'You're freezing.'

She always went cold when she had a panic attack, a result of her blood pressure dropping, but she wasn't about to explain that now. 'I'm fine—'

He stared at her for one long, fathomless moment, his arm gripping hers. He felt warm and steady and strong and the temptation to lean into him was nearly unbearable. She stood straighter.

'Let me get you a wrap. The nights are chilly here.'

'Fine.' Not that a wrap would actually help.

He came back a few minutes later with a matching lavender pashmina and draped it over her shoulders. 'Thank you,' Lindsay murmured, and they kept walking.

The quarter mile to the main villa felt like a trek across the Sahara, and yet Lindsay would have willingly walked it forever rather than face what was inside.

All too soon they had arrived; Lindsay paused before the huge double doors that led to the enormous marble foyer with its sweeping double staircase. Antonios greeted the manservant who opened the front doors, and then several other servants who circulated through the foyer, trays of canapés and glasses of champagne held aloft.

Definitely a casual dinner, then.

Lindsay managed to murmur a few hellos, offer some smiles. After a few minutes Antonios led her into the living room where his family waited; Lindsay saw his brother, Leonidas, by the window, Parthenope sitting on a sofa, her lips pursed and her eyes narrowed as she stared at her. Xanthe and Ava stood together by the window, heads bent together. Lindsay watched as one of them whispered something to the other.

Her chest constricted so much it felt as if she were having a heart attack. She stopped where she stood, flung one hand out to brace herself against the doorway as Antonios walked into the room to greet his family.

'Lindsay,' Daphne Marakaios said and, rising from her chair, she walked towards Lindsay, her arms outstretched.

Lindsay accepted the woman's embrace, felt how much thinner and more fragile she seemed from the last time she'd seen her. 'Daphne,' she murmured, and pressed a kiss against each of her mother-in-law's wrinkled cheeks.

Daphne eased back, her gaze sweeping over

Lindsay. 'It's so good to have you back, my dear.' She squeezed her hands. 'I hope it is good to be back?'

The questioning lilt in Daphne's voice made Lindsay wonder just how much her mother-in-law knew about the state of her son's marriage.

'Of course it is,' she murmured. It was good to see Daphne again at least, and she hoped her mother-in-law knew it.

'Come sit by me,' Daphne instructed, and led Lindsay to a sofa in the corner of the room. She was grateful for her mother-in-law's attention; it kept everyone else from besieging her with questions, even if she felt their speculative stares from across the room. Still, she'd got one of the worst parts of the evening over with: the grand entrance that being with Antonios had always entailed, that had always reminded her of those unbearable evenings with her mother's friends.

Daphne chatted with her briefly, asking surprisingly pertinent questions about her doctoral research; in Lindsay's experience most people's eyes glazed over when she started talking about the abstract details of number theory, but Daphne seemed genuinely interested.

And talking about mathematics was the most calming thing Lindsay could have done; explaining the impossible and even mystical beauty of transcendental numbers made her breathing slow and her body relax.

From across the room she caught Antonios glowering at her and her mind blanked.

'I find your work so fascinating, my dear,' Daphne said and Lindsay realized she'd just stopped speaking, maybe even in the middle of a sentence. 'You have such a lively mind, such a fierce intelligence.'

Lindsay smiled, or tried to, because the sincerity in Daphne's voice made her suddenly feel near tears. If she'd stayed, perhaps if she'd just tried harder, she could have developed a relationship with this woman that would have gone a long way to addressing the absence of a mother in her own life since the age of nine. Maybe she would have made friends with Antonios's sisters, rather than having them now staring at her stonily from across the room.

And just like that the panic swamped her again. She pressed one hand to her chest to ease the pain, and Daphne laid a hand on her arm.

'Lindsay, are you all right?'

'I'm fine.' Those two words had become her mantra. Lindsay forced herself to drop her hand from her chest and smile at Daphne. 'Sorry, just tired from the flight. But how are you? Antonios told me—'

Daphne smiled wryly. 'Then you know I'm not so well. But I've lived a good life. I have only a few regrets.'

Which was, Lindsay thought, an extraordinarily honest thing to say. Most people defiantly declared they had no regrets whatsoever.

And as for her? Did she regret marrying Antonios? Loving him, even if it hadn't lasted? Leaving him? All of it?

'Shall we go into the dining room?' Antonios asked. He'd crossed the room without her realizing it and now stood in front of her, his smile perfectly in place although the expression in his eyes was veiled. In his dark suit and crisp white shirt and navy silk tie he looked impossibly beautiful, everything about him reminding her of how happy she'd been with him. For such a little while.

Lindsay stood up and took his arm, grateful for the support even though she could feel Antonios's tension. His forearm was like a band of iron under her hand.

It wasn't until everyone was seated at the dinner table, the first course served, that the questions started. The interrogation.

Antonios's sister Parthenope began it. 'So, Lindsay, how was America?'

'Fine. Cold.' Lindsay dabbed her mouth with her napkin, pressing it against her lips as she took a deep breath.

'You were gone a long time,' Xanthe chimed in, her eyes narrowed, mouth pursed. They were suspicious of her. Angry, too. Antonios might not have told his family what had happened, but they clearly guessed some of it.

'Yes…I had to continue my research.' She forced herself to return her napkin to her lap, pick up her fork. Her knuckles shone white as she clenched it and she made herself relax her grip.

'I thought you could do this research anywhere.' This from Ava, who was the same age as her, twenty-six, yet now looked at her as if she were an alien and inferior species—a wife who had left her husband to do mathematical research. A freak.

'I can,' she answered, her voice seeming to echo in her own ears. Her chest was starting to hurt again. 'But I had a few things I had to wrap up in New York.'

'Then you're finished there? You won't be returning?' Parthenope again, her voice sharper this time, as she shot Antonios a concerned glance.

Lindsay swallowed. And swallowed again. She couldn't think of anything to say. She didn't want to lie, but telling the truth was just as unpalatable an option and would only invite more questions. More disapproval. She could feel everyone's stares on her and her vision started to swim.

'Lindsay's not quite done in New York,' Antonios said, his tone carefully bland. 'But she knows her home is here.'

At this Parthenope nodded approvingly because, unlike Lindsay, she was a good Greek wife and would never even imagine leaving her husband for six whole months.

Lindsay blinked back the dizziness and reached for her wine glass, but her hands were so icy and damp with sweat that the glass slipped from her fingers and fell to the tiled floor, shattering into a million pieces and splashing red wine all over the pristine white tablecloth and her dress.

A ringing silence ensued as a staff member sprang to attention to clean it up. Lindsay stared at the mess in horror, felt her head go light again as everyone's gaze swung to her and the enormity of the situation and just how much of it she couldn't handle crashed over her once again.

'I'm sorry,' she managed through her constricted throat.

'Not to worry, my dear,' Daphne said. 'It could happen to anyone.'

But it happened to me. Lindsay clenched her

hands in her lap, dug her nails into her palms and hoped the pain would distract her from the full-fledged panic attack she could feel coming on. Dizziness. Trouble breathing. Chest pain.

She'd tried so many different things to control the attacks while she'd been here. Breathing techniques, reciting prime numbers in her head, the desperate measure of alcohol. Nothing worked, and pain didn't either.

Spots danced before her eyes.

'Excuse me,' she murmured, and rose unsteadily from the table. She could see Antonios frowning at her but she was past caring. If she didn't leave now, she'd embarrass herself—and him—far more than this.

Somehow she made it to the bathroom. She doubled over the sink, rested her cheek against the cool porcelain. Her head spun and her chest hurt.

After a few long moments the dizziness thankfully receded and she started to feel a little better. She washed her face and blotted her dress as best she could. She looked, she realized, terrible. Her dress had a large red stain on the front from the wine. She couldn't go back into the dining room like this.

She sank onto the floor, drew her knees up to her chest and wondered whether she could spend the rest of the night—the rest of her life—in the bathroom.

A knock, an impatient *rat-a-tat-tat*, sounded on the door. 'Lindsay, are you in there?'

Lindsay pressed her face against her knees. 'Go away, Antonios.'

'Open the door.'

She almost laughed at that. He was like a bull-dozer, steamrolling over everyone and every-thing to get what he wanted. She'd been charmed by his determination when they'd met in New York; no one had ever showed such an interest in and desire for her.

Now she just felt tired. 'Please go away.'

'Are you all right?'

This time she did laugh, wearily. 'No.'

Antonios jiggled the door and then pushed his shoulder against it. The door sprang open, and Lindsay wondered if *anything* could hold out against her husband.

He swore at the sight of her sitting hunched on the floor, and then crouched down so they were at eye level and peered into her face. '*Theos*… what's wrong, Lindsay? Are you ill?'

'No, I'm not ill, Antonios.' She straightened, every muscle aching from the exertion of the panic attack and her own futile resistance to it.

'Then what—?'

And suddenly she was so very tired of it—of him not understanding, of her trying, perversely and at the same time, to explain and to hide. He wanted to know? Fine. He could know. Everything. And she didn't even care whether he believed her or not any more. 'I was having a panic attack,' she told him shortly. She washed her hands and face in the sink, even though she'd already done so once. At least it was something to do.

'A panic attack…' Antonios was staring at her in amazement.

'Yes, a panic attack. I suffer from a social anxiety disorder. Being in strange situations, or being the centre of attention, can cause me to panic.'

Antonios continued to gape at her. 'And you… suffered from this during our marriage?'

'Yes.'

'But you never—'

'Said? I tried, Antonios. I tried to explain, but you never wanted to listen.'

'I would have listened if you'd told me something like that!'

She eyed him wearily. 'Are you sure about that?'

He stared back at her, his expression unreadable. 'Let me make my apologies to my family,' he said finally. 'Will you be all right for a few minutes?'

'I'll be—'

'Fine? I'm not buying that one any more.' His voice was flat, toneless. 'Will you be all right?'

Lindsay let out a shuddering breath. 'Yes.'

Antonios stalked towards the dining room, fury coursing through him, although what or whom he was angry with he couldn't say. Wasn't ready to think about. He had a terrible feeling it was himself.

Six questioning faces turned to him as he came through the double doors. His mother, his brother, his three sisters, Parthenope's husband. Everyone had witnessed Lindsay stumble out of the room like a drunken bat out of hell, and the ensuing silence had been appalling.

'Lindsay's not feeling well,' he told them all. He kept his voice brisk, his face neutral. 'I'm taking her back to our villa.'

Daphne half rose from her seat, her face drawn in a frown of concern. 'Is there something I can do, Antonios?'

'No. She'll be—' *fine* stuck in his throat '—she needs to rest,' he said instead, and turned from the room.

Lindsay was exactly where he'd left her, in the bathroom, her hands braced against the sink, her hair falling forward to cover her face. 'We'll take a car back,' he said and she shook her head.

'I'm not an invalid. I can walk.'

'Even so.' She looked terrible—pale and sweaty, her hair tangled about her face. Seeing her like this made everything inside Antonios tighten like a giant fist. He wanted to protect her, to take care of her, to shout at her.

Why didn't you tell me?

It was a howl of anguish and anger, of guilt and grief, and he swallowed it all down. There would be time for that later, to ask questions and demand answers. Right now he just needed to take care of Lindsay.

He took her arm and led her from the bathroom, guiding and sheltering her, to the front steps of the villa where the car he'd arranged waited, one of the staff acting as driver.

He opened the door and helped her inside the car; she didn't resist. And then, with neither of them speaking, they drove off into the night.

CHAPTER FIVE

AS SOON AS they were back at the villa, Antonios strode to the en suite bathroom and starting running the tub. Lindsay stood in the doorway of the bathroom, exhausted and emotionally drained, knowing Antonios would expect answers and pretty sure she didn't have the resources right now to give them.

'Have a bath,' he said, and dumped half a bottle of expensive bath foam into the tub. 'Then we'll talk.'

A bath sounded heavenly and Lindsay was grateful for the reprieve from any conversation. Antonios left the room and she stripped out of her ruined dress and sank into the steaming water frothing with bubbles, feeling utterly overwhelmed.

For the three months of their marriage she'd kept it together better than that. She'd hidden it better, at least from his family, and even from Antonios. Now, the very first day, the first occasion she'd had to panic, she had. Utterly. She wondered what Antonios's family thought of her now. What he thought of her. She wished she was too tired to care, but the truth was she hated—had always hated—the thought of him knowing her weakness. It was what had made it so difficult to tell him in the first place. Now she felt a fist of fear clench in her stomach at the thought that he knew, even though it didn't matter. They didn't have a relationship any more.

After half an hour soaking in the tub she felt a little better, although wanting nothing but to sleep, and she got out and swathed herself in one of the huge terrycloth robes hanging from the door. She combed her hair and brushed her teeth and, with nothing left to do, she opened the door, throwing back her shoulders as she went to face Antonios.

He was sprawled on the sofa in the living room, a tumbler of whisky in one hand, the moonlight streaming through the sliding glass doors washing him in silver.

He turned his head to gaze at her fathomlessly as she came into the room; Lindsay braced herself for the questions. The accusations. He spoke only one word.

'Why?'

His voice was so bleak and desolate that Lindsay had to fight back an ache of regret and sorrow. 'Why what?' she asked and he took a long swallow of whisky, shaking his head.

'Why didn't you tell me?'

She sank onto the sofa opposite him. 'I've told you, I tried—'

'I don't recall ever hearing you mention agoraphobia, Lindsay.'

She plucked at a loose thread on the dressing gown. 'Maybe I didn't get that far.'

'And why didn't you? If I'd had any idea of how much you were suffering, I might have understood more. Listened more—'

'Listened more? You didn't listen at all, Antonios. You left for a business trip two days after we arrived in Greece.'

His mouth tightened. 'It was necessary.'

'Of course it was.'

'You never protested—'

'Actually, I did. I asked why you had to leave so soon, and you told me it was important. You practically patted my head before you left. Why didn't you just hand me a lollipop while you were at it?' The words surprised her, yet they felt right. Antonios's gaze narrowed.

'Are you implying that I was patronizing towards you?'

'Oh, well done, you get a gold star. Yes, that's exactly what I'm implying.' The anger she felt now took her by surprise. She was so used to feeling guilty and ashamed about her own deficiency, but this felt cleaner. Stronger. And she needed to be strong.

Antonios was silent for a long moment. 'I didn't mean to be patronizing,' he said at last. 'But I don't see how that has anything to do with you not telling me—'

'Don't you? Can't you see how it might be just a little bit difficult to tell your husband of one week that you have a debilitating condition when all he does is tell you over and over everything is going to be fine, just give it time, and insists you have nothing to worry about?'

'In normal circumstances, that would be true—'

'You think so? You think most wives get whisked off to a country where they don't speak the language—'

'Everyone in my family speaks English.'

'The staff don't. The staff I was meant to *supervise* for a dinner party less than a week after I arrived!'

The skin around Antonios's mouth went white. 'I thought I was giving you an honour, as mistress of the household, to plan—'

'Yet you never asked if I *wanted* to be mistress of your household. Never asked me what I wanted from life, from marriage.' She shook her head, weariness replacing her anger. 'Perhaps I should have spoken up more, Antonios. Perhaps I should have told you the truth more plainly. But I did try, even if you didn't see it.' She swallowed hard. 'I tried as hard as I could, considering how overwhelmed I felt.'

'Drowning,' he reminded her quietly, and she nodded.

'Yes, it felt like I was drowning. Like I couldn't breathe. Couldn't function—'

'And I didn't see this.' He didn't sound disbelieving, more just wondering. 'Did you have panic attacks like the one you had tonight when we were together?' She nodded, and he shook his head. 'How? How could I have missed that?'

'I tried to hide it, from your family. From you.'

'So you were trying to tell me and hide from me at the same time.'

Which made his aggravation understandable. 'I suppose I was.'

He let out a long, weary sigh and then leaned forward, his head bowed as he raked his hands through his hair. 'Tell me,' he said after a moment, his voice low. 'Tell me about your…condition.'

'You saw for yourself.'

'Tell me everything. Tell me how it started, how you've coped…' He looked up, his expression determined even as Lindsay saw an agony in his eyes. She ached for him, for herself, for them. If only things had been different. If she'd been stronger, braver. If only Antonios had listened more…

Or was it absurd to think things could have been different, that a mere action or word could have changed things for the better? The failure of their marriage hadn't happened, she knew, because of a simple lack of communication. It went deeper than that, to who they both were fundamentally and what they'd expected from life, from love.

But, even if their marriage was over, she could still give Antonios the answers he asked for. Maybe it would provide a certain sense of closure for both of them.

'I was always a shy child,' she began slowly. 'Definitely an introvert. I had a bit of a stammer, and I used to get stomach aches over going to school.' Antonios nodded, his gaze alert and attentive, more so than ever before, and she continued. 'My mother came from a family of famous academics. Her father was a physicist who travelled the world, giving lectures, and her mother was an English professor who wrote literary novels, very well received. I think she thought when she married my father, a mathematics professor, that her life would be like that.'

'And it wasn't?'

Lindsay shook her head. 'My father liked his work, but he didn't want to be some famous academic. My mother dropped out of graduate school when she fell pregnant with me, and I think maybe...maybe she resented me for that.'

Antonios frowned. 'Surely she could have gone back to school, if she'd wanted.'

'Maybe she did go back, eventually,' Lindsay answered. 'I wouldn't know. She walked out on me—on us—when I was nine.'

Antonios's gaze widened as it swept over her. 'You never told me that.'

'I suppose there are a lot of things I didn't tell you, Antonios.' Lindsay felt her throat thicken and she blinked rapidly. 'I don't...I don't like to talk about my mother.'

'So you became more anxious after she left?'

'Yes—but I was already suffering from panic attacks before then. She used to hold these sort of literary salons—she'd invite a bunch of academics over to our house and they'd talk about lofty things, books and philosophy and the like. It all went over my head. But she'd always call me into the room before bed and try to show me off, make me recite a poem or something in front of everyone. I think she wanted to prove to them she wasn't wasting her life, being a stay-at-home mother.'

'And you didn't like that.'

'I hated it, but I was also desperate to please her. I'd spend hours memorizing poems, but then when I got in front of everyone my mind would go blank. Sometimes I'd start to hyperventilate. My mother would be so disappointed in me she wouldn't talk to me, sometimes for days.' She still remembered sitting at the kitchen table, swamped in misery, while her mother maintained an icy silence, sipping her coffee.

Shock blazed in Antonios's eyes. 'Lindsay, that's awful. Didn't your father notice?'

'A bit, I think, but he was immersed in his research and teaching. And I didn't tell him how bad it was because I felt so ashamed.'

'And is that why you didn't tell me?' Antonios asked quietly. 'Because you felt ashamed?'

'Maybe,' Lindsay allowed. Her feelings about her anxiety and Antonios and their time in Greece were all tangled up—frustration and fear, anger and guilt. And, yes, shame. 'I've worked hard as an adult to control my anxiety, and even to accept it as part of me, but I know back then my mother was ashamed of me.' A lump formed in her throat, making the next words hard to form, to say. 'It's why she left.'

Antonios stared at her, his face expressionless even though his eyes blazed—but with what emotion? Anger? Pity? She hated the thought, even now, of him pitying her. 'How can you say that?' he asked in a low voice.

'My father finally noticed things weren't right when I was eight,' Lindsay continued, squeezing the words out past that awful lump. 'He took me to a specialist and had me examined and diagnosed. And he accepted a position in upstate New York, where I live now, far from Chicago, where we'd been living. My mother felt it was a demotion, and she didn't want to live in some poky town.'

'So she left because of that,' Antonios said. 'Not because of you, Lindsay—'

'I suppose it was the whole package really. The town, the house, the husband, the child.' She took a deep breath and met his gaze, the seventeen-year-old memory as fresh and raw as it ever had been. 'She came to New York to look at the house and college. We all went, and I remember how she walked around the empty rooms. She had this terribly blank look on her face and she didn't say anything, not until my father asked her what she thought, and then all she said was, "This isn't what I expected."' Tears stung her eyes, and one slipped down her cheek. Lindsay dashed it away. 'My father and I thought she meant the house, or maybe even the town. But she meant us. Life with us. It wasn't what she'd expected. We didn't make her happy.'

'She said that?' Antonios asked, his voice sharp with disbelief, and Lindsay nodded.

'She spoke with my father that night. I heard them from my bed. She said she couldn't cope, living in a place like this with…with a daughter like me. She said she was leaving.'

'Oh, Lindsay.' She was staring down at her lap by that point so she didn't see Antonios move, didn't know he had until his arms were around her and he'd pulled her onto his lap. 'I'm sorry. So sorry.'

'It was a long time ago,' she said with a sniff, but she couldn't keep the tears back, couldn't keep them from sliding down her face as Antonios wiped them away with his thumbs, just as he had back in New York when she'd told him about her father's death. He'd been so tender with her then, and he was so tender now.

'So you blamed yourself,' Antonios said quietly, one hand still cradling her cheek. 'For your mother's abandonment.' He was silent for a moment, one hand stroking her back. 'Were you afraid I might react the same way?'

'I…' She stilled, her mind spinning with that new and awful thought. Had it not just been shame, but fear, that had kept her from speaking honestly? Had she been afraid Antonios would reject her, even leave her if she told him the truth, the whole truth? Maybe some secret, sad part of her had. 'I don't know,' she said slowly. 'I know some deep-seated part of me hates anyone to know. I don't like you knowing now, even though it doesn't matter any more.' Thoughts and memories tumbled through her mind. 'I suppose I felt with you the same way I did with my mother. Wanting to hide my anxiety because I knew it made her angry, yet desperate at the same time for her to see it, to see *me*.'

'And I never saw you.' Lindsay couldn't tell anything from Antonios's flat tone. 'I only thought I did.'

What they'd felt for each other hadn't been real. It was no more than what she'd been telling him all along, yet it still hurt to hear him acknowledge it. To know how little they'd actually had together.

Antonios was silent for a long moment, one hand still cupping her cheek while the other stroked her hair. 'And so what happened after you moved to New York?' he finally asked.

'Things got worse. I think my father expected them to get better, but with my mother leaving…' She trailed off, then forced herself to continue. 'I started having panic attacks about school—being asked a question, being in a classroom. My father finally withdrew me when I was ten and I was homeschooled. I did all my lessons through a cyber academy, online.' It had been a relief, to leave all the stares and whispers of school, for everyone had realized she was different, that something was *wrong* with her, but it had made for a lonely existence. Her father had tried to be at home as often as he could but he hadn't possessed the resources or sensibility to enrol her in extra classes or activities so she could meet people, make friends. It had just been the two of them, rubbing along together, until he'd died.

'I graduated from high school when I was fifteen,' she continued. 'And started college early, which was hard at first. It made me realize that I had to start coping, that I couldn't hide from life forever. I started therapy and I worked hard to deal with my anxiety. It helped that I was studying mathematics. Numbers have always felt safe to me. They never change.'

'And so you managed for quite a while,' Antonios said. 'Studying and teaching.'

'Academia has always felt like a safe environment to me. I stayed at the same college for my BA and MA and PhD. I taught a few introductory classes, and I was actually okay standing in front of a classroom.'

'And then your father died,' Antonios recalled quietly.

'Yes. He suffered from early-onset dementia and I cared for him. Life became a bit limited because of that, but I didn't mind.' How could she have minded when her father had given up so much for her? Moved and sacrificed his marriage for her?

'It must have been hard.'

'Yes. And when he died I felt—lost. Adrift. I'd been in the same place for fifteen years but it was as if I didn't know anything any more. So I went to New York to escape everything, even myself, and I met you.'

'And I,' Antonios said after a moment, 'was the ultimate escape. The perfect fairy tale.'

'Yes.'

They were both silent, the only sound the draw and sigh of their breathing. 'I'm sorry I didn't know all of this before,' Antonios said finally. 'I'm sorry you didn't feel you could tell me.'

'I don't know if it would have made a difference, Antonios.'

He turned her on his lap so he could look her in the face. 'How can you say that? You were suffering—'

'I never should have married you,' Lindsay told him, even though it hurt to say it. 'I never should have come to Greece with you. I should have realized it wasn't real. That it couldn't work.'

Antonios didn't answer, and Lindsay wondered if he agreed with her. If she wanted him to agree with her. She felt tired and sad, the relief of having told him the truth coupled with a weary resignation that it didn't, after all, change anything.

'It's late,' he finally said. 'You should get some sleep.' He slid his hands up to cradle her face and pressed a kiss to her forehead. Lindsay closed her eyes, willing yet more tears away. It had been far easier to convince herself she'd never loved Antonios when he was arrogant and dismissive. It was much harder when he was so gentle. 'Thank you for telling me now, Lindsay,' he said softly and wordlessly she nodded. She was afraid if she spoke she would cry. Again.

He stared at her for a long moment, and then he tucked a stray tendril of hair behind her ear. He smiled sadly and Lindsay tried to smile back, but her lips wobbled and, knowing she was far too close to losing it completely, she slid off his lap and hurried from the room.

Antonios stayed in the living room, drinking far too much whisky as Lindsay got ready for bed. He could hear her in the bedroom, opening and closing drawers, the sensuous slide of material as she took off the robe.

He could imagine her, her alabaster skin, so creamy and smooth, the full, high breasts he'd held in his hands and taken into his mouth. Her slender waist and slim hips, those long legs she'd once wrapped around his waist. Her hair as soft and blonde as corn silk, spread out across his bare chest.

They'd been happy together, damn it, even if

just for a little while. And yet now he could no longer live in the little bubble of his own certainty. He'd been so damnably certain about how right he was. How *wronged* he'd been. He'd blamed Lindsay for everything, when he hadn't even noticed that she'd been struggling. Suffering.

Drowning.

He poured himself another whisky and tossed it back, needing the burn of alcohol against the back of his throat, in his gut. Craving the oblivion. He'd been blind before, of course. He'd been ridiculously, wilfully blind when it came to his father. He'd refused to see that anything was wrong, that Marakaios Enterprises was struggling. Just as he had with his marriage.

What the hell was wrong with him? Why couldn't he see what was right in front of his face?

Because you didn't want to see it. Because you were afraid.

Looking back, he could remember moments that should have given him pause. Moments he'd pushed aside because it had been easier. Lindsay claiming she had a headache, her eyes puffy and red. Excusing herself from a party or dinner table with sudden urgency. Yes, looking back, he could see that she'd been unhappy. He just hadn't wanted to see it at the time.

And now? What could he do now to make it better? He'd brought Lindsay back to Greece, back into the spotlight she despised. At least now he could try to make things easier for her. She might need to be here for his mother, but she didn't need to play hostess or be the centre of attention. He'd make sure of that. It was, considering all that had happened before, the least he could do for her.

It was nearing two in the morning by the time he finally made it to bed, his head aching from the endless circling of his thoughts as well as far too much whisky. He stopped in the doorway of the bedroom, his heart suspended in his chest as he watched Lindsay sleep. Her hair was spread out across the pillow, the colour of a moonbeam. She wore a white cotton nightgown with thin straps of scalloped lace, and Antonios could see the round swell of her breasts above the thin material as her chest rose and fell in the deep, even breaths of sleep.

Desire shafted through him, along with an almost unbearable sorrow. It was too late now. Too much had happened, too much hurt and misunderstanding. Their marriage really was over. Lindsay had made that clear.

Wearily, Antonios stripped down to his boxers and slid into bed. It was a wide king-sized bed but it felt too small as he lay on his back, trying not to touch Lindsay even though everything in him ached to pull her into his arms, remind her just how good it had been between them. That, he knew, would be a very stupid thing to do.

Eventually both the whisky and exhaustion overcame him, and he slept.

Lindsay awoke just before dawn, a pale greyish-pink light filtering through the bedroom curtains. She blinked, closing her eyes again as she sank back into the soft, sleepy cocoon of a feather duvet—and a hard body pressed against her own.

Her senses jarred awake even as her mind remained fogged with sleep. She could feel a masculine, muscular leg between her own, a hard chest squashing her breasts. *Antonios.*

Her body went on delicious autopilot, her arms sliding around Antonios's neck as she arched closer to him. Felt the hard press of his arousal against her thighs.

Memories rippled through her mind like reflections in water. Laughing with Antonios. Hugging him, feeling safe and protected and cherished. Making love with him.

She felt one large hand slide from her hip to the dip of her waist to finally, thankfully cup her breast, his thumb moving over the already taut peak.

She gave a breathy sigh of pleasure and Antonios moved her onto her back, his hands seeking her urgently now, lifting her nightgown, finding her flesh. One hand slid between her legs and she moaned and lifted her hips in invitation, wanting and needing to feel him inside her, to experience that wonderful sense of completion and wholeness again.

He was above her, braced on his forearms,

poised to slide so deliciously inside her, when the alarm bells that had started to clang distantly in her mind broke into furious peals.

She opened her eyes, stared straight into Antonios's face. He was staring at her with the same expression of appalled realization that she knew she must have on her own.

This shouldn't be happening.

She could feel the tip of his arousal brushing against her and it took everything she had not to arch her hips upwards in invitation.

With a groan Antonios flung himself away from her, rolled onto his back, one arm covering his eyes. Lindsay lay there, her nightgown rucked up to her waist, everything in her aching, demanding satisfaction. With a shuddering breath she pulled down her nightgown and rolled onto her side.

'I'm sorry,' she said hesitantly.

'Don't be.' Antonios lowered his arm and gazed up at the ceiling. 'We both got carried away.' He sat up, throwing off the sheets, and strode, magnificently naked, towards the en suite bathroom. 'We're due at the main house for breakfast with my family,' he said over his shoulder, his tone flat. 'But if it's easier for you, we can have breakfast here and then visit my mother privately.'

His thoughtfulness only hurt her more. 'I think I can manage breakfast.'

He turned to look at her, his eyes narrowed. 'Don't push yourself, Lindsay, on my account.'

'It's fine, Antonios. I know what I'm capable of.'

He nodded in wordless acceptance and disappeared into the bathroom. Lindsay sank back against the pillow. If Antonios had been this sensitive and understanding before, would their marriage have survived? It was a hard question to ask, and an impossible one to answer.

The morning when she'd decided she was going to leave him, her body had felt like a leaden weight, her mind nothing but buzzing emptiness. At that point, after enduring three months of near-constant scrutiny from his family while being routinely ignored by her husband, her anxiety had been nearly all-consuming.

She'd barely been able to drag herself to luncheons and dinners, parties and receptions, all planned for Antonios to introduce his new wife to the local community, to his world. All the while she'd tried to hide the stress-induced eczema on her hands and eyelids, the nausea that had her rushing to the bathroom at inopportune moments, the migraine headaches that came out of nowhere, the light-headedness and shortness of breath that had plagued her every time Antonios took her somewhere public.

The attacks had been worse than anything she'd ever experienced before; she'd been in a strange environment and, far worse, with a man she thought she'd loved but who suddenly seemed like a stranger. She'd been lonely and lost and utterly miserable.

Escaping had felt like her only option for survival. She'd woken that morning and known she no longer possessed the strength, either physically or emotionally, to continue. She couldn't drag herself to one more lunch or dinner, couldn't try to have one more fruitless conversation with Antonios. It had all felt, quite literally, impossible.

And so she'd left. Not telling him she was leaving had been the coward's way out, Lindsay knew, but she simply hadn't had the strength to explain anything any more. She'd told him she needed to return to New York to wrap up some things with her father's house. Antonios had asked her how long she'd be gone and she'd prevaricated, telling him she'd book a return ticket when she was done. He thought she'd be gone a week.

On the plane back to New York she'd felt like a zombie, an empty shell. She'd barely heard the stewardess asking her if she wanted something to drink or eat. She'd simply stared straight ahead, her mind and body going into a kind of emotional and mental hibernation.

Then she'd stepped across the threshold of her father's house; she'd still been able to smell the scent of his pipe and suddenly she'd burst into tears. She wasn't even sure what she was weeping for: her failed marriage, her father, dead just four months, her own weakness that had wrecked so much in her life. Everything.

With a heart that felt like a dead weight inside

her she'd typed out the pithy email to Antonios, telling him their marriage was a mistake and she wasn't coming back. He'd called that afternoon and she'd heard the bewilderment and anger in his voice, had felt it when he'd hung up on her. At least she'd chosen to leave, she'd told herself, and then she'd curled into a ball on her bed and slept for fourteen hours straight.

And waded through the next few weeks, trying to summon the strength to rebuild her life. And she had, or at least she'd started to. She'd started therapy again and returned to her research. She'd met up with a few friends who hadn't asked too many questions about her brief failed marriage, and she'd told herself it was enough.

It had to be enough.

Lindsay rolled onto her back and stared up at the ceiling as she heard the sound of the shower being turned on. She imagined Antonios naked under the spray, rivulets of water streaming down the taut perfection of his body.

The body she'd almost just taken into her own, the body she knew as well as her own. The body she missed so much.

Because the little life she'd built for herself back in New York hadn't been enough. Not remotely, not when she'd tasted true happiness with Antonios.

It wasn't real, she reminded herself. *It didn't last*. Letting out a long weary sigh, Lindsay rolled out of bed.

They got ready for breakfast without speaking or even looking at each other. Lindsay showered and changed into a pale green sundress and sandals, plaited her hair into a French braid.

Antonios was wearing chinos and a white linen shirt open at the throat, the light-coloured clothes making his skin and hair seem even darker. He looked magnificent and the sight of him freshly showered, the scent of his aftershave, made desire spiral dizzily inside her again.

Desire she would have to control. Neither of them could afford another encounter like the one they'd had this morning.

His gaze flicked over her as she emerged from the bedroom but he said nothing and they walked in silence to the main villa.

Just as before, everyone was assembled in the

dining room as they arrived, and six pairs of eyes trained on Lindsay as she walked into the room. She felt the speculation, even the censure, and once again her chest went tight.

This time, though, Antonios didn't stride ahead, oblivious. He reached for her arm, steadied her elbow, his body half shielding her from the stares of his family. She glanced up at him in surprise and saw him gazing back at her with that steady strength that had drawn her to him when they'd first met. Antonios had felt like the rock she could cling to in the drowning sea of her own fears and anxieties. He felt that way now, and she was touched by his sensitivity. Despite everything that had happened last night, she hadn't expected it.

After a few seconds her breathing returned to normal and with a little nod she walked forward; Antonios dropped his arm and went to pull out her chair.

'I hope you are feeling better this morning, Lindsay?' Daphne asked as one of the staff poured Lindsay some of the thick Greek coffee she'd learned to drink and even like while she was there before.

'Yes, I think so. Really, I was just tired.'

Ava and Parthenope shot each other significant looks and Lindsay wondered why that remark would set Antonios's sisters off. Deciding not to care, she focused on eating her breakfast of fresh fruit and yogurt with honey, and thankfully the conversation swirled around her without her needing to contribute to it.

'Would you like to go back to the villa?' Antonios asked as they left the dining room. 'I need to work this morning.'

'I suppose.' She could check her email and do some work on her research. She glanced at Antonios, wished she knew what he was thinking about everything. What she'd shared last night. What they'd nearly done together this morning.

Clearly none of it had changed anything between them—but had she wanted it to? The question jarred her because she didn't want to ask it, much less answer it.

'You'll be all right?' Antonios asked when he'd dropped her back off at the villa.

'I have an anxiety disorder, not a life-threatening illness,' Lindsay answered a bit sharply. 'You don't have to coddle me, Antonios.'

'I'm just trying to be considerate,' he returned. 'Since I wasn't before.'

His thoughtfulness made guilt twist inside her. 'I'm sorry,' she said. 'This is hard for me.'

'I know, Lindsay. And I'm trying to make it easier.'

'I don't mean that. I mean having you know about my condition. I hate seeming weak.'

He raised his eyebrows at that. 'You think you seem weak? I think you're strong. Amazingly strong, to have managed as much as you have, and coped for so long.' He smiled with a painful wryness. 'I think you're strong for having been able to hide so much from me, but maybe I was just too blind to see it.'

'I think we were both to blame, Antonios.'

'Maybe so.'

They stared at each other for a moment, regret etched on both of their faces. Then, her heart aching, Lindsay turned to go inside.

She fetched her laptop from her carry-on bag

and Antonios retrieved his phone and shrugged on a blazer before heading out once more.

'I'll see you later,' he said and Lindsay watched him go, wishing all over again that things were different between them…and knowing they never could be.

CHAPTER SIX

ANTONIOS SPENT THE morning working in his office but he had trouble focusing on anything. His mind once more was on Lindsay, and all the things she'd told him last night.

As well as what had happened this morning. Dear heaven, but it had felt so good to have her in his arms once again. It had taken every ounce of his control not to slide inside her, not to take his pleasure and give her her own.

And yet what a paltry pleasure it had turned out to be. Good or even incredible sex wasn't enough to make a marriage. And he accepted now that their marriage had made Lindsay miserable. Guilt and grief weighed heavily inside him at the thought.

After Lindsay left him, he'd been so consumed with self-righteous anger. So certain it was all her fault, that he'd done everything in his power to make her happy. He'd bought her clothes and jewels, had showered her with physical affection, had brought her into his home and his family, and he'd thought that had been enough. He knew now it hadn't been, and never could be.

He attempted to focus on work for another hour but thoughts about Lindsay were bouncing around his brain like the little ball in a pinball machine and he finally gave up and headed out into the sunshine of a fall afternoon. He walked back to the villa with no clear goal in mind other than seeing Lindsay again. What he would say to her, he had no idea. What was there left to say?

He came into the cool shelter of the villa, stopping in the doorway to watch Lindsay unobserved. She was sitting on the sofa, her slender legs propped up on the coffee table, her computer on her lap. She was frowning at the computer screen, utterly intent, a few tendrils of hair having escaped her plait to frame her face in white-blonde curls. She was, he saw with a sudden surge of affection, mouthing something silently.

'You look incredibly engrossed in what you are

doing,' he said and, startled, she jerked her head up, her body tensing as she caught sight of him.

'Just some research.'

She'd told him a bit about her research before, but Antonios hadn't really understood it. Hadn't tried to, he supposed, because he'd been showing her his life, not having her show him hers. He'd been incredibly selfish, Antonios thought with a fresh bout of recrimination. Incredibly self-centred and arrogant, assuming Lindsay could just drop her life and friends without a thought. He'd felt, he realized, as if he were rescuing her, and he'd liked that, liked feeling like someone's salvation. And instead he'd caused the destruction of her happiness.

'Tell me about it,' he said now, and he came to sit on the edge of the coffee table. He had an urge to reach out and touch her, wrap a hand around the slender bones of her ankle. He resisted.

Lindsay looked up at him warily, her gaze narrowing. 'Do you really want me to?' she asked.

'I wouldn't have asked otherwise.'

'Okay, but you never…' She stopped, shrugging, and then explained, 'At the moment I'm working on maximal prime gap function.'

'Okay,' Antonios said, although he didn't actually know what that meant. Lindsay gave him a lopsided smile, as if she guessed as much, and he smiled back and shrugged.

'I might need you to explain this in plain English.'

'It's all Greek to you?' she teased softly and his smile widened. He was enjoying their light banter. It certainly made a change from the endless arguments they'd had lately.

'Something like that. You must be used to people not understanding your research.'

She gave him a rueful nod and smile. 'Most people don't.'

'So…maximal prime gap function. Give me the low-down.'

She laughed softly, and the sound was the sweetest music to Antonios's ears. He'd missed her laugh, her happiness. Knowing he was causing it now, if just a little, was a balm to his soul. To his heart. Maybe he could use this week to make up for the unhappiness he'd caused her during their marriage. If he could make her laugh again, or even smile…

'Well, you know what prime numbers are?' she said, and he had to think for a moment to dredge up the arithmetic he'd learned as a child.

'A number that is only divisible by itself and one.'

'Yes. The prime gap is the difference between two prime numbers. A maximal gap is the greatest difference.'

'So, for example, the difference between three and seven.'

'Yes, although I'm working with numbers far higher than that—numbers that have yet to be determined if they're in fact prime.'

'And have you drawn any conclusions?'

She shook her head. 'Not yet. I'm still gathering data. But when I have enough I'll start to look for patterns.'

'What kind of patterns?'

'Similar gaps between primes mainly.'

'And what will that tell you?' Antonios asked. 'About…anything?'

She let out a laugh, no more than a breath

of sound, her smile turning rueful. 'I know—it seems completely useless to you.'

'Not useless,' he replied. 'But I must admit, as a businessman, I prefer to deal in practicalities.'

'Understandable.'

'So what will the patterns tell you?'

'Well…' Her fingers splayed over her keyboard, a faint frown puckering her forehead. 'Maybe nothing; maybe everything. That, really, is what draws me to number theory. The more research scientists do in physics and mathematicians in number theory, the more they realize how much we don't understand. But the research provides little glimpses into a world of knowledge—a world defined by numbers, and to me it is both mystical and beautiful.' She smiled self-consciously, but Antonios was intrigued.

'Defined by numbers?' he repeated. 'What do you mean?'

'Well, for example, cicadas.'

'Cicadas?'

'Yes, you know, like grasshoppers?' She smiled, her eyes dancing with amusement, turning to silver.

'What do cicadas have to do with prime numbers?'

'In the eastern US they only appear after a prime number of years. For example, in Tennessee cicadas have a thirteen-year life cycle. In other places they only appear every seventeen years.'

'And you think there is a reason for this?' Antonios asked, mystified.

'Science has shown us again and again that things in nature are rarely arbitrary. In the case of cicadas, having an irregular life cycle means they're avoiding their natural predator population cycles. So cicadas on a thirteen-year life cycle are less likely to be gobbled up by a frog.'

'How would they know that?'

She shrugged, smiling. 'They wouldn't, necessarily. It's most likely part of natural selection. But I certainly find it interesting. Why have cicadas adapted and other insects haven't?'

'Maybe they're smarter than we think.'

Her eyes danced some more. 'Maybe.'

'Fascinating,' he said, and meant it. 'But the

research you're doing, with these huge prime numbers. How does that apply?'

'It doesn't, yet. But with the advances being made in technology and quantum physics, it could in years to come. Understanding the relationships between numbers could be the key to unlocking the universe.'

Her mouth curved in a teasing smile and Antonios chuckled. 'You think so, huh?'

'Actually, I do, in a manner of speaking. But it probably sounds weird to you.'

'Not as weird as it did.'

She laughed and closed her laptop. 'Then my job here is done.'

'Good,' Antonios said. 'Because I thought we could go for a walk.'

She raised her eyebrows, searched his face, wondering, no doubt, why he was being so friendly. He'd been angry for so long. Too long. But he'd enjoyed the last twenty minutes and he wanted to spend more time with Lindsay. Wanted to make her smile again.

'Okay,' she said, and Antonios rose from where he'd been sitting.

'You should put on sunscreen and take a hat.'

'Where are we going, exactly?'

'To the olive groves.'

As a child he'd loved the olive groves that spread across the hillside, all the way to the horizon. He loved the twisted, gnarled trunks of the olive trees, and the pungent smell of their fruit as it ripened. He loved the crumbly earth beneath his feet and the high, hot sun above. And most of all he'd loved walking with his father, feeling important as his father had pointed out the different trees and flowers.

Until everything had changed.

He knew, just as Lindsay did, how a parent could make you feel confused and ashamed. Unloved and rejected.

They walked through the complex of buildings that made up Villa Marakaios, passing the main villa as well as Leonidas's, the staff housing and the central office, before coming to the wrought iron gate with *Marakaios* worked into the iron in curling script above them, in both Greek and English. Antonios opened the gate and ushered Lindsay into the grove.

'So how did your family get into the olive oil business, anyway?' she asked as they walked between neat rows of trees, their grey-green leaves rustling in the wind, the tight cream-coloured buds of their flowers raised to the sun.

'It was my father,' Antonios said, and heard both the tension and pride enter his voice. He had such conflicting feelings when it came to his father. Respect and disdain. Anger and grief. Love and hate. 'He came from nothing,' he told Lindsay. 'His father lived in Athens and worked as a dustman. But my father had dreams and ambition, and he loved the earth. He sweated blood to buy some land, and over the years he expanded it. He decided to grow olive trees for oil because he felt it was something that would always be in demand.'

'And he was very successful.'

'Yes,' Antonios said, 'although not at first. It can be very expensive to make olive oil unless you make it in large quantities using efficient methods. My father struggled at first, but then he was able to buy more land and plant more trees.'

'And so you inherited an empire.'

Antonios's insides tightened with memory. 'Yes,' he agreed. He had sworn never to tell anyone about how the Marakaios empire had been crumbling beneath his feet when he'd been summoned home after his father's heart attack. He wouldn't tell Lindsay. He'd protect his father's memory as he always had, even though it sometimes felt as if he were selling his soul to save his father's.

He still remembered coming home after starting a job in Athens—a job his father had insisted he start because he hadn't wanted him near the family business. Hadn't wanted him to figure out just how badly things were going. Antonios hadn't realized that at the time, though. He'd just felt the rejection.

Just like he had with Lindsay. God help him, he didn't want to be blind any more. He wanted to see what was happening around him, and to help. And he would this week with Lindsay.

'What are you thinking about?' Lindsay asked and Antonios snapped his gaze back to her.

'Nothing.'

'You're frowning.'

He shrugged. 'I was just thinking about all there is to do.'

'Taking time out to go to New York was costly, I suppose.'

'But necessary.'

Lindsay didn't answer and they walked on for a bit, the sun hot on their heads and shoulders even though the air was still cool and crisp. The aromatic scent of the olive flowers wafted up from where they trod over fallen buds.

The grove stretched in every direction, a sea of land and trees that gave him a fierce, almost painful sense of satisfaction. He'd held onto it all, if only just. He might have sold his soul, but at least he'd saved this. Lindsay turned to him with a small smile.

'You look like a king surveying his domain.'

'I suppose I feel a bit like one,' he admitted. 'I am very proud of what my father built from nothing.' And what he'd kept, if only by the skin of his teeth.

Lindsay laid a hand on his wrist, her fingers cool and soft. 'I'm glad you showed me all of this, Antonios. It helps me to understand you.'

He gazed at her, conscious of her hand still on his wrist, her lovely grey eyes so wide and clear. 'And do you want to understand me?' he asked quietly.

Her eyes clouded and she withdrew her hand from his arm. Antonios felt the loss. 'I…' she began, and then shook her head. 'I suppose there isn't much point, is there?' she said, her lips twisting in a sorrowful smile. 'But I'm still glad.'

Antonios just nodded. He felt emotion burn in his chest, words rise in his throat and tangle on his tongue. Too many memories, too close to the surface. Too much hopeless longing and unsatisfied desire.

Their marriage, he reminded himself grimly, was over.

'We should get back,' he said. 'My mother is hoping to have us over to the main villa for lunch.' He glanced at her sideways. 'Just the two of us. Will that be all right?'

'Fine,' Lindsay assured him. 'I'm all right in small groups of people. And I like your mother, Antonios. I like being with her.' Her expression clouded once more as she turned to him. 'I'm so sorry about her illness.'

He nodded, his chest tightening once more. 'I am, too.'

'I'm…I'm sorry I wasn't there for you when she was diagnosed.' She bit her lip. 'I know I should have been.'

Antonios struggled for words for a moment; the emotions that swooped through him were too powerful and overwhelming for speech. He couldn't untangle one from the other: gratitude and compassion, hope and sorrow. He wished she'd been there. He wished she'd wanted to be there, had been happy there.

'You're here now,' he said. 'That's what matters.'

They started walking back the way they'd come. 'When will you tell your family that we're getting divorced?' Lindsay asked and Antonios tensed.

'When the moment is right. Are you in such a rush?'

'No, but are you really going to keep up the deception for the rest of your mother's life?'

'That won't,' he answered, 'be all that long. The doctors have only given her a few months or maybe even weeks. The cancer has spread, and she doesn't wish to undergo invasive treatment again.'

'Do you want me to tell her?' Lindsay asked quietly. 'I owe you that much, at least.'

'No.' His voice came out too loud, too hard. 'It would only hurt her. Why can't we let her die happy, believing we're happy?'

Lindsay nibbled her lip. 'I don't like lying.'

'I don't either.' And God help him, he'd been doing it for too long. But for a greater good, just like now. 'It would be a mercy for her, Lindsay,' he said quietly. 'Why trouble her in the short time she has left?'

Lindsay gazed at him, her eyes shadowed, and then slowly she nodded. 'All right. But what about your sisters and brother, Antonios? They seem suspicious already—'

'After,' Antonios said, his voice hoarse and raw. 'I'll tell them after she dies.'

Lindsay's face crumpled and she reached out for Antonios's hand, seeming to surprise both of them. She squeezed his hand, her face filled with compassion. 'I'm so sorry, Antonios. Daphne has been more of a mother to me than my own ever was.'

'We'll both miss her,' he agreed, his voice still hoarse. He didn't want to let go of her hand. Didn't want to resort to this careful politeness and wary friendship. Maybe what they'd had before hadn't been real, but it had been good. And maybe they could build something real now.

The thought was like a dagger slipping inside him, slyly finding his heart—and hurting. Because he knew he couldn't suggest such a thing to Lindsay. Not when being here with him had only caused her unhappiness. He owed her her freedom, at the very least.

Lindsay followed Antonios out of the olive grove, reluctant to leave behind the surprising camaraderie they'd shared. She'd enjoyed chatting with him, teasing and sharing, learning about one another. It was more than they'd ever done before during the three months of their marriage. The week in New York had been one of sensual rather than emotional discovery, and then during those months in Greece they'd been like strangers unless they'd been in bed. But today they'd actually felt like friends.

It made her feel both sad and happy at the same time, because while friendship with Antonios was better than the hostility she'd experienced over the last few days, it still made her ache with regret and longing.

They walked to the villa in companionable silence, and then Lindsay went into the bedroom to change. She exchanged her sundress for a pair of linen trousers and a matching sleeveless top, and touched up her make-up and hair.

Antonios was waiting for her in the living room when she emerged and his gaze fastened on her as soon as she opened the door.

'You look lovely,' he said, his voice full of warm sincerity as his gaze swept over her.

She blushed, although she wasn't sure why. He'd told her she'd looked lovely before, had showered her with compliments, but this felt different. And then Lindsay knew why. Because for the first time Antonios truly saw her…and he still thought she was beautiful.

The realization made her understand afresh why she hadn't told him about her anxiety. She really had been filled with shame and fear, terrified that he would reject her or even leave her. She'd convinced herself that she'd tried her best to tell him, but she really hadn't. She hadn't wanted to.

'Lindsay?' He came forward, one strong hand cupping her elbow. 'Are you okay?'

'Yes—'

'You look pale.'

She shook her head. 'I was just realizing how unfair I was to you, Antonios, not telling you the truth. I told myself I'd tried as hard as I could, but I know I really didn't. Because I really didn't want you to know.'

'Between a rock and a hard place,' Antonios surmised with a small sad smile. 'We were doomed, weren't we?'

'I suppose we were.' Which made her feel like bursting into tears. Wanting to hide her emotion, she turned away from him, making a pretence of straightening her top. 'We should go. Your mother will be waiting.'

They walked over to the main villa where Daphne was waiting for them. Lunch had been set out for the three of them in one of the villa's smaller dining rooms, with French windows overlooking a small walled herb garden. Lindsay had never been in the room before and its cosy proportions and atmosphere put her immediately at ease, as did Daphne.

'How are you settling back into life in Greece?' she asked as she took Lindsay's hands in her own thin ones. 'Is it very hard?'

Lindsay swallowed, hating to deceive her, yet knowing as Antonios had said it was both a mercy and kindness. 'Not too hard.'

'And I hope you're treating her right,' Daphne said with a stern look at her oldest son. 'Antonios works too hard,' she told Lindsay. 'He's just like his father that way.'

Lindsay felt the shudder of tension go through Antonios's body and wondered at it. She slid him a glance, but his face was impassive as he held out a chair for his mother.

Daphne took a seat, smiling up at Antonios. 'Evangelos was always working. I used to come into his office and sit on his desk.'

Lindsay let out a choked laugh and Antonios's eyebrows shot up. 'I didn't know that, Mama.'

'Why would I tell you?' she asked with a surprisingly pert look. She turned back to Lindsay. 'But it was the only way to make him stop working.'

'Maybe I should have tried that,' Lindsay joked, then bit her lip as she registered the past tense. Her gaze locked with Antonios and she knew he'd registered it, too.

'It would make for an entertaining change from what's usually on my desk,' he said smoothly. 'Let me pour you some water, Mama.'

This was going to be so hard, Lindsay thought, busying herself with spreading her napkin in her lap. Pretending at a party was one thing, but to someone's face, someone she cared about…

'Let me call for the first course,' Daphne said. 'I'm afraid I don't last for more than a few hours before I need a nap these days.' She smiled apologetically and Lindsay touched her hand.

'I'm sorry…' Lindsay began. 'If there's anything I can do…'

'There is no need for you to be sorry,' Daphne said. 'I've lived a good life, and I'd rather no one made concessions to my condition now. I want to live life as fully as I can for as long as I can.'

One of the staff came in to set the first course before them, a fruit salad with grapes and succulent slices of melon.

'Tell me, Lindsay,' Daphne asked as soon as the staff member had quietly left again, 'do you miss America very much? Did you leave many friends behind?'

Lindsay couldn't help but glance at Antonios, whose face was carefully expressionless. 'Not so many,' she said.

'And your research? Will you be able to finish it here? You are not far from achieving your doctorate, are you?'

'I have a few more months of work at least,' Lindsay answered. 'Most of the research can be conducted from anywhere, as long as I have my laptop.'

'I'm sure you will have to make some trips

back to America,' Daphne said, and Lindsay nodded in relief.

'Yes, I will.'

'Not too many, though,' Daphne continued. 'A man and a wife belong together.' She speared a slice of melon, her gaze suddenly seeming almost shrewd. 'Six months apart is a very long time.'

Lindsay threw a panicked gaze at Antonios, not sure how she should answer.

'Lindsay had some business to deal with, back in America,' he said, his voice as smooth and controlled as ever. 'With her house and such things. Her place is here now, Mama, with me.'

'And why couldn't your place be with her?' Daphne countered, a playful smile curving her mouth. 'In America?'

Antonios's composure slipped for a second as he stared at his mother, slack jawed. 'Because I can't run Marakaios Enterprises from America,' he said finally.

Daphne nodded, her playful smile turning down at the corners. 'No,' she agreed softly, 'you can't.'

* * *

Antonios pushed his plate away, wishing this meal could be more pleasant for all of them. Deceiving his mother so directly was far more difficult than he'd envisioned, and he could tell Lindsay was finding it hard, too.

As for his mother's suggestion he leave Villa Marakaios…the idea was absurd. He'd poured his soul into the family business, had sacrificed all semblance of a normal life to keep things afloat. He couldn't walk away from it, even if he wanted to.

Thankfully, Daphne moved the conversation to more innocuous matters as they ate their way through three courses, and Antonios was glad to leave contentious matters aside as they chatted simply. He liked watching Lindsay, the way her eyes sparkled when she was amused, the way she tilted her head to one side when she was considering a point. The clear peal of her sudden laugh made him long to make her laugh again. Make her happy again, even if just for this week.

By the time dessert had been cleared Antonios

could see that his mother was fading and so he made their excuses, kissing her on both cheeks, as Lindsay did after him, before they left the main villa to head back to their own.

The afternoon air was still and drowsy, the grounds silent and empty in this hot part of the day.

'Are there any more engagements today?' Lindsay asked and Antonios shook his head.

'No, but there will be preparations for the party tomorrow, and then the actual celebration the day after.' He glanced at her, wanting to be considerate but knowing she would resist being coddled. 'Will that be all right for you?'

'I think so.'

'I want to make things easier for you,' he said, his manner stilted yet sincere, the awkwardness of it making him cringe inwardly. 'But I know you don't want me to treat you differently, either.'

'You're being very kind, Antonios. I appreciate all you're doing for me.' For a moment she looked as if she wanted to say something more and Antonios felt his heart lurch with fear and hope. Then she shook her head, her eyes shadowed as she touched his hand. 'Thank you,' she said, and walked on to the villa.

CHAPTER SEVEN

LINDSAY TILTED HER face to the sun and closed her eyes, enjoying the warmth—as well as the respite from the preparations for Daphne's party. Even though Antonios had insisted she didn't need to, she had joined his sisters in the villa's main salon to help with the decorations.

Antonios was so clearly making an effort to help her, she felt she could do no less and help him. And if they'd had this kind of understanding before, would it have made all the difference? Could their marriage have survived, or even flourished?

Restlessly, she shifted in her seat, plucked a blossom of bougainvillea that twined its way up the stone wall. That question had been tormenting her in one form or another since she'd told Antonios about her anxiety. Maybe they'd needed to come to the brink of disaster to truly start listening and understanding each other. Maybe they'd needed the heartache and separation to come to a place where they could build something strong and true.

And maybe you're just spinning another fairy tale. Another fantasy.

She pressed the blossom to her cheek and closed her eyes once more. Even if she and Antonios understood each other now, even if they became friends, a marriage still couldn't work between them. She couldn't be the kind of wife Antonios needed, the social hostess and organizer. No matter how much she managed to control her anxiety, the endless social engagements his career as CEO demanded would still defeat her. And what of her own research? She'd told Antonios she could do her research anywhere, which was true. But her PhD would be finished in a few months and she'd already started looking for professorships. Staying here in Greece meant kissing her career goodbye.

Something she hadn't cared about or even considered when he'd asked her to marry him, to come with him to Greece. She'd been so desperate then—desperate to be happy, to leave the sadness of her life behind. But, nine months later, she could acknowledge how incompatible their life goals really were.

Antonios had stated plainly he would never leave Greece. Even if he wanted to restart their marriage, it would mean staying here, doing her best to be the wife he needed, playing hostess and socialite. Roles she couldn't bear.

'May I join you?'

Lindsay opened her eyes to see Daphne standing in front of her, offering her a kindly smile.

'Of course.' She shifted on the bench to make room for her mother-in-law.

Daphne sat down with a sigh of relief. 'Everything aches,' she said quietly, her gaze on the mountains cutting a jagged line out of the horizon. 'I think, when it is my time, I will be ready for the aching to stop.'

'I'm sorry,' Lindsay said quietly. She felt inadequate for the moment, especially in the light of Daphne's grace in the face of so much suffering and sorrow.

'Knowing you are going to die shortly is, in

some ways, a gift,' Daphne said after a moment, her gaze still on the mountains. 'It gives you a chance to set your affairs in order and say things you might have resisted before.' She turned to Lindsay, a surprising humour lighting her eyes. 'Speak the truth of your heart, because it doesn't really matter if you ruffle a few feathers.'

'I suppose,' Lindsay agreed after a second's pause. She had a feeling Daphne was going to speak a few truths now and she had no idea what she'd say in return.

'I know,' Daphne began, choosing her words with care, 'that things went wrong between you and Antonios.'

Shock blazed through her, followed by a deep unease. If she admitted the truth, would Antonios be angry? Was she to lie even now?

'I also know,' Daphne said, patting her hand, 'that Antonios doesn't want me to know. He tries to protect me from so much.'

Lindsay swallowed hard, searched for words. 'He loves you very much.'

'And I love him. I want him to be happy.'

Daphne was silent for a moment. 'I think you can make him happy, Lindsay.'

Lindsay shook her head, the movement instinctive and utterly certain. 'I can't. I know I can't.' Too late she realized how much she'd admitted, but her mother-in-law seemed unsurprised.

'Why don't you think you can?'

'Because I'm not what he needs. I can't be the kind of wife he needs.'

'I think,' Daphne answered, 'Antonios doesn't know what he needs.'

Curious now, Lindsay asked, 'What do you think he needs?'

'A wife who loves him. Who believes in him. You love him, don't you?'

'I…' Lindsay shook her head. 'I don't know. I thought I did, and then I thought I didn't. And now…now it doesn't matter.'

'Why not?'

Lindsay bit her lip. She'd said far too much. She'd been startled into more honesty than she'd ever meant to share. 'I only mean because we're already married,' she said feebly and Daphne smiled, as if she knew what a pathetic pretence this was.

'You weren't happy here,' she said after a moment. 'Were you?'

'No,' Lindsay admitted after a second's pause. 'But that was as much my fault's as—'

'A husband's duty is to make his wife happy, no?'

'I suppose a husband and wife should try to make each other happy—'

'Let me say again,' Daphne corrected. 'If a wife is unhappy, a husband needs to address her unhappiness.'

Lindsay swallowed hard. 'Antonios didn't know I was unhappy.'

'Exactly. I could see it and he could not. Because he is just like his father, Lindsay. He only sees what he wants to see.' Daphne let out a long weary sigh. 'Evangelos was a good man and I loved him dearly. But he worked himself to the bone for his business and he closed his eyes to any problems because he could not bear to think of them. Just as Antonios closed his eyes to your suffering because he could not bear it.'

Lindsay blinked, taking this in. It was an entirely new thought, and one she had to sift over for a few moments before replying. 'His eyes aren't closed now,' she said, half-amazed at how honest she was being. 'We've talked about it since I've returned. He knows everything. I'm not sure it makes much difference.'

'Because you still are not happy here,' Daphne said quietly. She sounded sad.

'Because, I told you,' Lindsay said sadly, 'I can't be the wife he needs.'

'And I told you that what he needs is to love and to be loved. That is all anyone needs.'

'You make it sound so simple.'

'No, not simple. Endlessly complicated and difficult.' Daphne smiled, resting one bony hand on top of Lindsay's. 'But worth it, if you both resolve to try. To learn.'

Lindsay swallowed and nodded. She wanted to believe Daphne, wanted to believe love could be that easy. But the question remained: did she want to try again? And, more importantly, did Antonios?

Antonios stared at his brother and tried to mask his shock. 'So you kept this from me?'

'I wanted to make sure it was a definite go,'

Leonidas answered, his voice level. The brothers stared at each other, tension simmering in the air.

Antonios glanced back down at the file folder of information Leonidas had presented to him ten minutes ago, much to his stunned amazement. The neat rows of figures and the printed transcript of correspondence showed his brother had been planning this investment in providing luxury bath products to a chain of hotels for a long time. Without telling him a damned thing.

'And it never occurred to you,' he asked, an edge entering his voice, 'to tell me you were thinking about doing this?'

'No, it didn't,' Leonidas answered flatly. Antonios jerked back.

'Do I need to remind you that I'm the CEO of this company?'

'No,' Leonidas interjected, 'you certainly don't.'

Antonios stared at his brother, felt a ripple of shock at the anger he saw there. 'What is that supposed to mean?'

'Exactly what I said. You remind me every

day that you're the boss, Antonios. That's why I didn't approach you about this plan. I knew you'd want to take it over.'

Antonios's gaze narrowed. 'As CEO, it's necessary that I—'

'Have your fingerprints on everything? And why is that, Antonios? I am your second-in-command, the Head of European Operations, a Marakaios.' His mouth twisted bitterly. 'He was my father, too.'

Antonios slapped his hand on the desk, the sound loud in the taut stillness of the office. 'Damn it, I do not need this now.'

'Fine. We won't discuss it. Just sign off on the deal and I'll go to our investors.'

'No.' The word came out in a sudden, sharp cry. Leonidas raised his eyebrows. Antonios's jaw tightened. He had, he knew, kept his brother on a short rein because he'd been hiding the extent of the debt their father had amassed. He'd cleared it now, but if Leonidas went to their investors, if he looked at their bank statements or credit history, he would know in an instant how bad things had been. How their father had failed.

And Antonios had promised never to let anyone know.

He'd kept Leonidas busy wining and dining new clients, visiting factories and restaurants, drumming up new business. He'd always handled the money side, but now Leonidas had gone behind his back, set up an entire new deal that he, quite naturally, wanted to close.

And Antonios couldn't let him.

'I'll sign off on the deal,' he said tersely, 'and I'll contact the investors.'

Leonidas's mouth twisted. 'Taking the glory, as usual.'

As if he concerned himself with glory. As if there was anything *glorious* about the debt and despair his father had fallen into, the life Antonios had lived for far too long. 'You can have your name on it,' he said shortly. 'I'll give you credit. But I'll handle the finances and paperwork.'

Leonidas stared at him for a long moment, his face taut with fury. 'Don't you trust me?'

'This isn't about trust, Leonidas.' At least not the kind his brother thought.

'Then why won't you give me more responsibility, Antonios? Damn it, I deserve it. I've worked hard these last ten years—'

'What responsibility do you want?' Antonios snapped, irritation masking his guilt. 'To sign some tedious paperwork, go over a few boring columns?'

'If it's so boring, why won't you let me do it?' Leonidas countered.

Antonios stared at him, hating that they were having this confrontation and yet knowing it had been a long time coming. Fearing he couldn't hide forever. And wouldn't it feel good to come clean, to admit what he'd been covering up, sharing the burden? Lindsay had been honest about her own fears and secrets. Why couldn't he be honest about his?

The desire to unburden himself was so strong he nearly trembled with the force of it. Longed to give Leonidas all the responsibility he craved and more, to walk away from it all, finally free of the shackles of Marakaios Enterprises that had bound him for so long…

Theos, what was he thinking? Appalled, Antonios took a step back, as if he could distance himself from his own thoughts. He could not betray his father that way. It would be a betrayal of himself, of his sense of duty and honour that was at the core of who he was.

'Be happy with what I've offered,' he told Leonidas flatly. 'Because it's all I ever will.'

With a muffled curse Leonidas strode from the room. Antonios pushed back from his desk, striding to the window that overlooked the olive groves. His mind seethed with too many thoughts.

He had never seen his brother so angry before, seeming so resentful of the control Antonios exerted. He'd sensed it, but Leonidas had never spoken so plainly before. Or maybe he hadn't wanted to acknowledge how unhappy his brother was, just as he hadn't wanted to acknowledge how unhappy Lindsay had been. Blind, wilfully blind, as always.

Antonios pressed a fist to his forehead, longing for so much to be different. For his father not to have sworn him to secrecy. For him to have realized the unhappiness around him and sought to change it.

And if only he could change things now. Change things with Leonidas. Change things with Lindsay.

Wearily, he dropped his fist and turned back to his desk. Sometimes change was impossible.

After talking with Daphne, Lindsay went back into the villa, determined to make one more attempt to help with the party preparations. Parthenope and Xanthe were in the salon, debating where to put a display of photographs; Lindsay watched them for a moment before coming over to examine the photos of the Marakaios family throughout the years.

She could pick out Antonios easily—a dark-haired, solemn little boy. For a second she imagined what their child might have looked like and felt an unsettling twist of longing for something she hadn't even truly considered before.

Antonios had wanted to start trying for children right away, but Lindsay had put him off. Attempting to cope with her new life in Greece had been hard enough without adding pregnancy to the mix.

And it was still hard. Too hard to continue. Too hard to try again.

She turned to watch Xanthe and Parthenope continue to wrangle over the display board, their voices raised, their hands moving wildly.

Xanthe caught her looking and put her hands on her hips. 'Do you have a suggestion, Lindsay?' she asked, a faint note of challenge in her voice. Parthenope turned to look at her, too, and even though it was just the two of them Lindsay felt a sweat break out between her shoulder blades.

Damn it, she did not want to go into panic mode right now.

'I'd put it in the corner,' she said, and Xanthe's eyebrows shot higher.

'People won't see it there.'

'It will be in the way anywhere else,' Lindsay countered quietly, 'and a person's gaze is generally drawn to the vertex of an angle, especially a right angle.' She saw the look of incomprehension on the two women's faces and felt herself flush. 'The walls of the room form an angle,' she explained in a half mumble. 'A right angle, with the corner as its vertex.'

They just stared at her, completely nonplussed, and Lindsay turned away. 'Never mind,' she muttered, and everything in her jolted with surprise when she heard Antonios's voice.

'A mathematical proof for putting photographs in the corner. Brilliant.' He came into the room, his smiling gaze trained on Lindsay, rooting her to the spot. 'I knew I needed a reason to have the photo of me as an eight-year-old with knobbly knees put in a dark corner.'

'You could backlight the display board,' Lindsay offered, pleasure rippling through her as Antonios joined her, looping one arm around her shoulders. 'Your knobbly knees could still be on view.'

'You did have knobbly knees, Antonios,' Parthenope remarked as she peered at one of the photos. 'Are they still so knobbly? You always wear business suits now.'

'I'll never tell,' Antonios answered, and slid

Lindsay a teasing glance. 'And I trust my wife will keep my secret.'

'My lips are sealed,' Lindsay promised, but inwardly she reeled. Why was Antonios acting so…*lover-like*?

Then it hit her. He was pretending, for his sisters' sake. *Duh*. How could she have forgotten it for even a moment? How could she have wanted something real?

She slipped out from under Antonios's arm. 'I don't think my mathematical proofs are really needed here,' she said with an apologetic smile for Parthenope and Xanthe. 'I'll just head back to our villa.'

'I'll join you,' Antonios answered smoothly. 'I'd like to rest before dinner.'

Lindsay saw Xanthe and Parthenope exchange knowing looks and inwardly cringed. Outside, she started walking quickly towards the villa and Antonios easily matched her pace.

'It's too hard, Antonios,' she burst out. 'Pretending to everyone. It feels wrong.'

'I know.'

This stopped her short. 'Then shouldn't we come clean? Wouldn't it be easier?'

'For whom? Us? Think of my mother, Lindsay.'

Lindsay bit her lip. 'I think your mother knows. Or at least guesses.'

Antonios turned to her sharply. 'Why do you say that?'

'Because she spoke to me this morning. Privately. And some of the things she said made me think she knows. She knew I was unhappy, anyway.'

Antonios's mouth thinned. 'Which was more than I knew.'

Lindsay stopped to lay a hand on his arm. 'What happened before, we should both put behind us, Antonios. I know we were both to blame. We can accept our guilt and move on.'

Something flared in his eyes. 'Move on?'

'I mean, you know…move on with our lives,' Lindsay stumbled through the explanation. A blush heated her cheeks as she thought what Antonios might have assumed she meant. To move on together.

Antonios didn't answer, just stared at her for a long moment, his gaze seeming to both test and assess her. 'Have dinner with me tonight,' he said suddenly.

Lindsay stared at him in surprise. 'I thought we were having dinner with everyone, at the main villa—'

'No. Have dinner with just me. Alone.' She searched his face, saw how intent and determined he looked. As determined as he had when he'd asked her out in New York, his playful banter not quite disguising his utter intent to have her go out with him, to have her fall in love with him. And she had. Oh, she had. She'd fallen for him so hard and fast her head had still been spinning a week later, when they'd landed in Greece.

And what did he want now? What did she even want him to want?

'Antonios…'

'Please,' he said softly, and she was lost. As lost as she'd been when he'd given her that achingly whimsical smile of his and said, *What would it take for you to have coffee with me?*

And she'd grinned and said, *A simple please would do.*

And so he'd said it. Tears stung her eyes and she blinked them back, everything in her aching for what they'd had and lost.

And what they could have again?

Hope was such a dangerous thing.

'All right,' she whispered and Antonios's answering smile reached right into her soul.

Antonios paced the living room as he waited for Lindsay to emerge from the bedroom for their dinner. Nerves coiled in his belly and anticipation sang in his blood. He'd planned everything, from the food they'd eat to where they'd eat it, the music that would be playing and the flowers on the table. He wanted this evening to be perfect, and focusing on all the details had kept him from thinking about all the things that could go wrong.

Like Lindsay telling him no.

But that wouldn't happen. He wouldn't allow it to happen. He'd pulled himself back from the brink once before, by sheer force of will and a hell of a lot of hard work. He could do it again. He was, he knew, willing to work hard for his marriage. And it would begin tonight.

'I'm ready.'

He turned to see Lindsay standing in the doorway, looking both uncertain and beautiful. She was dressed in a silvery, spangled sheath dress, her hair loose and tousled about her shoulders.

'You look like a moonbeam,' Antonios said and came forward to take her hands in his. 'Or a Snow Queen, perhaps.'

She gave him a faint smile, and he knew she remembered him calling her that when they'd met in New York. His Snow Queen. For she would, God willing, be his still.

'Where are we eating?' she asked as she glanced around the empty, darkened villa.

'Somewhere private. I made arrangements earlier. It's only a short walk away. Do you have a wrap?'

She held up a scrap of spangled silk and Antonios took her arm in his.

Outside, the night was dark, the air crisp, the sky scattered with stars like a thousand diamond pinpoints in a cloth of black velvet. Lindsay took a deep breath.

'I love the smell of the air here,' she said. 'So fresh and clean. It smells like pine.'

'From the trees on the mountains,' Antonios told her. 'The villagers used to harvest the pine resin.'

'The resin? For what?'

'Well, it's edible,' Antonios told her, 'but I wouldn't advise eating all that much of it. Mainly it was used to make pitch and other adhesives.'

She slid him a smiling glance. 'And you didn't think about going into the resin business?'

'I'm not sure pine resin has all that much value these days, with all the chemical adhesives available now.'

'Did you always want to take up the family business?' Lindsay asked after a moment, and Antonios tensed.

'It was never a question of want.'

'You mean your father expected you to?'

'Of course. He built an empire. He wanted to hand it down to his sons.' And he hated talking about this, about the lies that he knew he'd get tangled up in.

'So you've always worked for Marakaios Enterprises?'

'I worked for an investment management company in Athens briefly, when I was younger. My father wanted me to have some other experience.' That, at least, had been what Evangelos had told him. The truth had been he'd wanted him out of the way.

'And did you enjoy that? The investment management?'

'Yes, I did,' Antonios said, and heard the note of surprise in his voice. He'd never really thought about the work he'd done in Athens, only the hurt he'd felt about being sent away. But the truth was he'd enjoyed it very much. Enjoyed the analysis coupled with risk-taking, and the freedom of not having another man's burden on his shoulders.

'What about you?' he asked. 'Your father was a mathematician. You taught at the same university he did. Did you ever think about doing something else?'

'No. Never,' she answered. 'Mathematics has always been my passion, and I've never been very good at starting somewhere new.' She swallowed and looked away and it occurred to him afresh how difficult it must have been for her to come to Greece, an entirely new place, with him.

And he hadn't made it one iota easier for her. But he would this time. He'd make sure of it.

'Here we are,' he said and, taking her elbow, he guided her into the extensive walled gardens of the estate. They walked in silence along several twisting paths, the gravel crunching under their feet, until they came to a private little garden surrounded by stone walls climbing with bougainvillea, a fountain in its centre, the water gleaming under the moonlight.

Lindsay stopped as she took in the preparations Antonios had made: the table set for two with fine china and linen, candlelight flickering over the silver chafing dishes. A bottle of champagne was waiting on ice in a silver bucket and a recording of a double concerto for violin and cello was playing softly in the background.

'Brahms' Concerto in A Minor,' Lindsay said

softly. Remembrance suffused her face; they'd seen the New York Philharmonic play this at Carnegie Hall in New York, after Lindsay had told him it was one of her favourite pieces of music. 'The musical A-E-F is a permutation of F-A-E,' she'd explained to him, amusing him with her mathematical way of looking at everything. 'It stands for his personal motto: *Frei aber einsam*.' Her mouth had twisted as she'd translated, 'Free but lonely.'

Now he understood how those words must have resonated with her. And with him, too, he thought now—working so hard to save Marakaios Enterprises, hiding the truth from everyone. Until he'd met Lindsay and felt his soul start to soar.

And it would soar again. Both of theirs would. He could make it happen.

'This is very thoughtful, Antonios,' Lindsay said quietly. 'And very romantic.'

'That was my intention,' he answered as he pulled out her chair. She sat down with a whisper of silk and he laid the napkin on her lap before sitting down opposite her.

Lindsay's gaze was shadowed as she looked at him. 'This is lovely, Antonios,' she said. 'So lovely, but…'

'But why am I doing it?' he filled in before she could say anything more.

She nibbled her lip, her eyes wide. 'Yes.'

'Because I want to,' he answered her simply. He took a deep breath, meeting her gaze, knowing his heart was in his eyes. 'Because I still love you, Lindsay, and I want you to stay in Greece.' He smiled, or tried to, for her expression hadn't changed. 'I want us to stay married.'

CHAPTER EIGHT

LINDSAY STARED AT ANTONIOS, saw sincerity blazing in his eyes as his words echoed through her. *I want you to stay in Greece... I want us to stay married.*

I want. I want.

And nothing about what she wanted. What she needed. What she'd felt, all those weeks in Greece. She took a deep breath, felt sorrow sweep through her; she was too tired and sad to be angry. She felt only disappointment at the realization that, as much as he was trying, Antonios still hadn't changed. Still couldn't see.

And yet she wanted him to. Wanted this to work, even though she knew it couldn't. *She* couldn't.

'You're speechless?' Antonios said with a little laugh. 'Say something, Lindsay.'

'I don't know what to say.'

'Say you want that, too, then,' Antonios answered. He was trying to speak lightly, but she could hear an edge entering his voice, signifying what? Irritation? Impatience? She wasn't falling all over herself to say yes.

'Oh, Antonios,' she said finally. She shook her head, and his mouth tightened. 'It's not that simple.'

'I think it seems quite simple. I love you. Do you love me?' He tilted his chin a bit, as if bracing himself for a hit.

Lindsay stared at him miserably. 'I don't know,' she said finally, but she knew it was a lie. She wouldn't feel this terrible, this torn, if she didn't love him. 'I do love you, Antonios,' she said, the words drawn from her reluctantly because she knew they would only make him insist all the more. 'But it's not enough.'

'Of course it's enough.' Triumph blazed through his voice and Lindsay closed her eyes briefly.

Daphne's words had been rattling around in her head all afternoon. *To love and to be loved... is all anyone needs.*

If only that were true. But she was all too afraid it wasn't, at least not for them. Not for her.

'I know what you're thinking,' Antonios said and Lindsay's eyes flew open.

'Do you?' she asked.

'You're wondering how it will work, with your condition.'

She stilled, wondering just how he intended to fix this. Control it, because that was what Antonios did with everything.

'A bit,' she allowed.

'I've thought about that,' Antonios continued, leaning forward, the untouched meal before them momentarily forgotten. 'We can make concessions, Lindsay.'

'Concessions,' she repeated, and knew she hated that word.

'Adjustments,' he amended. 'We'll curtail your appearances at public events. We can live separately from everyone else, in our own villa. We can even limit family engagements, although I hope in time you might come to accept—'

'Stop, Antonios—' she cut him off, unable to listen any more '—just stop.'

He sat back, confusion and irritation chasing across his features. 'I thought you'd be pleased.'

'That you're willing to make so many *concessions*?' she finished and his mouth tightened.

'It's just a word.'

'No, it's not.' She shook her head, slumping back in her seat. 'I don't want you to make concessions, Antonios. I don't want you to have to put up with me.'

'I'm not putting up with you—' he cut her off, his voice sharp '—I told you I loved you. I want this, Lindsay. I'm trying to be considerate.'

'I know you are,' Lindsay said. 'But it's not enough, Antonios. I'd only make you unhappy because I'm not what you want, not really.'

'Maybe you should let me decide what I want.'

'And you really want a wife who hides in the shadows, who can't be by your side?'

'In time—' he began and she shook her head almost frantically.

'No. No. I don't want you to try to *fix* me, Antonios.'

'You said yourself you've worked hard to control your anxiety. I just want to help you.'

Lindsay closed her eyes. 'So I can fulfil a role I never even wanted or asked for.' He was silent at that and she opened her eyes. 'In any case, you'd only become frustrated and disappointed. Because I'd never be good enough.'

'Let me decide that.'

'No, I won't, actually. I won't agree to a half life here that dwindles away to nothing when you decide you're done with me—'

'I wouldn't,' he shot back, his voice rising to a roar. 'I would never abandon a marriage.'

'Like I did?' The hurt spilling from her didn't make sense. She was so angry and so sad, and it felt as if nothing could make things better.

'Like your mother did,' Antonios answered. 'Because life wasn't what she expected. Was that why you left, Lindsay? Because life wasn't what *you* expected?'

She felt the blood drain from her face, empty from her head. 'I can't believe you said that.'

'Damn it, I'm trying to fight for our marriage. To find a compromise. What is so wrong about that?'

'Because the compromise rests on the assumption that I have to stay here in Greece and try to be your perfect little wife,' Lindsay snapped. 'And you never even asked if I wanted that.'

'I'm a traditional man,' Antonios answered tightly. 'Naturally I would expect my wife to have her place with me. And you told me you wanted to go to Greece, that there was nothing left for you in New York.'

'And I've told you since then,' Lindsay reminded him, 'that I was feeling particularly lonely and vulnerable when you asked me. But the truth is, Antonios, I did have a life in New York. Maybe it was a small one, with just a few friends, a little job. But I liked it. I don't want to give that all up just to be a shadow of the woman you want.'

They stared at each other, the anger and tension between them palpable in the cool night air. Antonios threw down his napkin on the table.

'*Theos*, I don't know what I can do,' he muttered, raking a hand through his hair.

Lindsay stared down at her plate as she blinked back tears. Maybe she was being unreasonable. Unfair. Antonios had created this lovely romantic dinner, was trying to find ways to make her—*their*—life in Greece possible. And she just kept insisting it wouldn't—couldn't—work.

Maybe she needed to give a little. Find a way to make their marriage, their life together possible. Antonios was willing to be flexible; surely she could be, too. She could look into professorships at universities in Grecce, or even do some private tutoring. Something. If she loved him she would try, wouldn't she?

Try to be someone you really aren't? Was that what love was?

'I never considered that coming to Greece would be difficult for you,' Antonios finally said, the words drawn from him slowly. 'I was so eager to bring you here, to have you share in my life. Because I was lonely, too, Lindsay. I needed you, even if you didn't think I did.'

Lindsay's throat had thickened so it hurt to get the words out. 'Antonios…'

'And I want you to want to share it,' he continued. 'But you don't.'

Lindsay felt a tear slide down her cheek. 'It's not that simple.'

'Isn't it?' He gazed at her bleakly. 'Isn't it, Lindsay? You don't even want to try.'

Because I'm afraid of failing. Because I'm afraid you'll reject me, hurt me, leave me.

The realization was painful in its clarity. This wasn't even about expectations, or living here, or whether she could teach in Greece. It was about fear—a fear she'd held on to since she was nine years old and her mother had walked out on her because she hadn't been enough.

She was so afraid of that happening again. More afraid than she'd ever admitted to herself.

She remembered when Antonios had asked her to marry him, to go with him to Greece.

They'd been lying on the huge king-sized bed in his suite at the Plaza, their legs tangled together, their hearts still beating fast from the lovemaking they'd just shared.

Antonios had twined his fingers with hers, ran his other hand up her bare thigh, resting it on the curve of her hip. 'I never thought I'd fall in love like this,' he'd told her, his voice husky with emotion. 'I never thought I'd be so lucky.'

Lindsay had blinked back tears as she'd answered, 'I never thought I would, either.'

'We're the luckiest people in the world,' he'd said with a smile before kissing her softly. And she'd agreed with him. She'd felt as if she'd won the lottery when she'd met Antonios. She'd felt like the most loved, adored and cherished woman in the world. After her lonely life, it had been the most incredible feeling.

And it had felt even more incredible when he'd risen onto his knees and taken her hands in his. 'I love you, Lindsay, more than anything. Will you be my wife?'

She'd seen the love shining in his eyes, felt it in herself. She hadn't had to think for so much as a millisecond before answering. 'Yes, Antonios. I'll marry you.'

They'd got married the next day, at a register office by special licence. It had been crazy and impulsive, and maybe that was because they'd both known that if they'd told people, Lindsay's colleagues or Antonios's family, someone would have talked them out of it. Advised them to wait.

And if they had waited?

Maybe they wouldn't be married after all.

But they were married, and they did love each other. And maybe that really could be enough.

'I never felt like I was good enough for my mother,' she told him slowly, haltingly. 'I felt like I always disappointed her, and that made me more anxious than anything else. She used to give me the silent treatment after I'd let her down. Once she didn't talk to me for a week.'

Antonios's face twisted with both sympathy and grief. 'And that was terrible, Lindsay. A terrible, terrible thing to endure.'

'And it affected me more than I'd ever let myself realize,' Lindsay continued. 'But I know now I can never let myself feel that way again. I can never let someone make me feel that way again.'

Antonios's expression darkened. 'And I would never do that to you.'

'But don't you see, Antonios, how it is?' Desperation edged her voice and her hands curled into fists at her sides. 'I don't fit in here. I can't be the kind of wife you need—'

'Maybe you should let me decide that.'

'I don't want you to have to make *concessions—*'

'It was just a word, Lindsay, just a stupid word!' He rose from his chair, took a step towards her. 'I love you. I fell in love with you in New York, on a snowy afternoon. Maybe it was fast and crazy but it was real, no matter what you said or tried to convince yourself of. What I felt for you, what I feel for you now, is *real.*' His voice throbbed with sincerity, the low growl of it reverberating through Lindsay's chest. 'And my love—our love—will be enough. I'll make sure of it. I won't let you down, I swear. I'll listen. I'll *see.*'

He looked so earnest and determined, and she wanted to believe him so badly. Was fear going to keep her from finding her happiness with this man? Would she let it?

'Lindsay.' He rose from his chair, came and dropped to his knees in front of her as he took her hands in his. 'Trust me. Please.'

Trust him. Trust him with her happiness as well as with her fear. With her heart and with her soul.

'You're asking a lot, Antonios,' she whispered.

'And I'll give a lot. I promise.' His hands tightened on hers.

She stared down at him, this proud, passionate man who was on his knees, begging for her. For her to love him. Her throat was so tight she could barely get the single word that she knew she meant, even if she was still afraid.

'Yes.'

He looked up at her, a fierce light of hope dawning in his eyes. 'Yes…?'

'Yes, Antonios, I'll try.'

With his eyes still blazing he pulled her face towards his, catching her up in his arms and then kissing her as if he would never stop.

And she never wanted him to.

CHAPTER NINE

AS ANTONIOS'S MOUTH crashed down on Lindsay's, he realized how long it had been since he'd kissed his wife. They hadn't kissed yesterday morning when they'd almost made love. They hadn't kissed, he realized as his tongue plundered the silky depths of her mouth, since she'd said goodbye to him in Greece.

And now she'd said yes. Yes to their marriage, to their love. Yes to him. Triumph and need surged through him and he deepened the kiss, turned it into a demand. He wanted her to give him everything now, not just a hesitant yes from her mouth but a passionate cry from her body. Yes. *Yes.*

In one fluid movement he pulled the silvery dress up and over her head. She gasped softly, her skin pale and pearl-like in the wash of moonlight.

'Antonios…' she whispered, and his name ended on a soft moan as he kissed her again, his hands sliding over her body, remembering the wonderfully familiar feel of her. From the moment he'd first touched her, he'd felt how they fitted, two halves of a whole beautifully joined. Now, as he drew her slender curves towards his, he felt it again, that inalienable rightness of the two of them together. And Lindsay must have felt it, too, for she returned his kiss, her body yielding to his in every way possible.

She shuddered under his touch, his fingers finding her secret places as her head fell forward in surrender, her hair gleaming in the moonlight.

'You love me,' Antonios said fiercely and she let out a trembling laugh.

'I already told you I did.'

'Say it again,' Antonios demanded, needing to hear it. To believe it.

'I love you,' she told him, her voice choking. 'I love you, Antonios.'

And, with triumph roaring through him, Antonios kissed her again.

* * *

If he was trying to prove to her how much she loved him, Lindsay thought hazily, he was wasting his time. She knew she loved him. And he set her body on fire. There had never been any question of that.

Already sparks were spreading out from her centre as Antonios kissed his way down her body, his hands cupping her breasts, thumbs teasing the already taut peaks. Need coiled tightly inside her, everything in her straining for the satisfaction only he could give her.

She gasped his name as she pulled at his shirt, craving the feel of his bare skin against hers. Fingers fumbling, she unbuttoned his pants, tugging them down from his hips.

Antonios pulled her onto his lap and she straddled him, his arousal pressing against the soft juncture of her thighs.

The desperate need to have him inside her overwhelmed her, drove out any rational thought. She sobbed his name as he positioned her above him and then drove into her, her legs wrapped around his waist, his name a ragged cry torn from her lips.

Afterwards they remained wrapped around each other, Antonios braced against the stone fountain, Lindsay cradled in his lap with her legs around his waist.

'We look like a Lissajous curve,' she murmured against his shoulder and Antonios eased back to smile wryly at her.

'A what?'

'A figure eight, I suppose,' Lindsay explained. She gestured to their legs: his stretched out and hers pretzeled behind his back. 'A Lissajous curve is the graph of parametric equations that describe complex harmonic motion. It looks a bit like a figure eight.'

'Complex harmonic motion,' Antonios repeated thoughtfully, lightly rocking his hips against hers. 'That sounds about right.'

Lindsay laughed softly and rested her head against his shoulder, breathing in the tangy masculine scent of him. She felt utterly sated, both physically and emotionally. *Complete*. The resistance she'd kept up for so long had been swept away, just as Antonios had swept her away in New York.

She had no idea what the future would look or feel like, and dwelling too long on the possibilities and pitfalls made fear clench her belly. But, no matter how afraid she might feel, she no longer fought against the future. Against Antonios and her love for him. His love for her.

What they shared, she thought as she pressed a kiss against his bare shoulder, was impossible to fight.

Antonios adjusted their bodies so he could look into her face. His eyes blazed with ferocity and yet his smile was tender. 'No regrets?' he asked softly and she smiled back.

'No. Some reservations, maybe. But no regrets.'

'It will work out, Lindsay. I swear it.'

And she knew that Antonios was the kind of man who would refuse all obstacles. Who would make things happen by sheer force of will. And maybe, for once, that was a good thing.

Tenderly, Antonios scooped her up from the fountain and carried her back to the table.

'Our dinner awaits.'

'I'm naked,' she pointed out, and Antonios gave a negligent shrug.

'I don't mind.'

She laughed, happiness rising inside her like a bubble. 'I'm also cold.'

He let out a theatrical sigh. 'Well, if you must,' he said, and scooped up her underwear and dress. Instead of handing them to her, he dressed her himself, slowly and lingeringly, so by the time he'd tugged up the zip on her dress Lindsay was nearly melting again with desire. 'Later,' he promised, and with one last soft kiss he led her back to the table and, with her heart brimming with happiness, Lindsay sat down to eat. She found she was suddenly starving.

Antonios left the bed, sunlight streaming over Lindsay as she lay tangled amidst the silken sheets, her hair spread over the pillow like a moonbeam. In sleep she looked relaxed and happy, her mouth curved in a small smile, one hand flung, palm upwards, by her face.

Antonios luxuriated in the simple pleasure of

watching her and knowing she was his. Finally. Again. *His.*

Last night, after they'd made love, they'd spent several pleasant hours eating their delayed dinner and chatting in an easy way that he wasn't sure they'd ever experienced before, not even in those heady days in New York, when everything had been an odyssey of discovery. Certainly not in Greece, which in hindsight he could see had been marked by strain and silence. This was new, and all the more precious because of it.

They were building something good now, he told himself. Something new and strong. And he would make sure it worked. His mouth hardening in a line of resolve, he turned from Lindsay lying asleep in their bed.

The sun was rising in a bright blue sky, the olive groves sparkling under its light. He wanted to wake Lindsay up before he left for work, make love to her again, but he knew he needed to get to the office. He had a staff meeting in a few hours, and he still needed to talk with Leonidas.

Just the thought of his brother had Antonios's insides tightening in a familiar and unwelcome way. For ten years he'd lived with that tightening, the unrelenting pressure of leading his father's business away from the precipice of disaster while keeping it all from his family.

When he'd met Lindsay in New York and fallen in love with her, it had felt like the first time he'd truly relaxed or been happy. And even though he now had that again he couldn't ignore the tension that ratcheted inside him as he scrawled her a note and walked across the estate to Marakaios Enterprises' offices.

He needed to talk to Leonidas. He hadn't realized the extent of his brother's resentment. They'd been close growing up, getting into similar scrapes on the estate, sharing the usual boyish escapades. United, perhaps, in the alienation they'd felt from their father, who had been consumed by the business he'd eventually run into the ground.

Thinking about his father made Antonios's chest hurt. He loved his parents, his family, and as any Greek man he was fiercely loyal to them. Even acknowledging his father's faults to himself felt like a betrayal and he forced down the stress that felt as if it had a stranglehold on his soul.

'You're late,' Leonidas remarked, unsmiling, as Antonios came into the reception area of the office. Antonios suppressed a flicker of irritation as he walked past his brother into his office, its floor-to-ceiling windows overlooking the olive groves now dazzling in morning sunlight.

'I didn't realize you were waiting for me,' he said. He dropped his briefcase by his desk, shed his suit jacket and sat down before opening up his laptop.

Leonidas stood in front of his desk, arms folded and chin jutting. 'I want more control, Antonios.'

Antonios didn't look up from his laptop. He wasn't surprised by Leonidas's demand, but he still didn't know how he was going to deal with it. 'You're Head of European—'

'Don't fob me off with that,' Leonidas snapped. 'I'm not a dog to be tossed a bone. In the ten years since you took over, I've never had access to financial information. I've never had any true authority. I'm nothing more than a front man who's meant to do the fancy talk.'

'And you're so good at it,' Antonios pointed out, spite spiking his voice even though he'd meant it to be flattery.

'Well, I'm done with being patronized,' Leonidas stated. 'You either give me more control or I leave.'

Anger surged through Antonios and he rose from his chair, one hand flat on the desk as he glared at his brother. 'Are you threatening me?'

'Simply stating a fact.' They glared at each other and in some distant corner of his brain Antonios wondered how it had come to this.

Because your father made it happen.

'I wonder,' Leonidas continued coolly, 'why you insist on hiding the financial information, Antonios.'

'Our accountant is completely up to date—'

'And you never let me in on those meetings. You've never let me so much as look at a spreadsheet. What are you hiding, I wonder?'

It took Antonios a stunned second to realize what his brother was implying. That he was cooking the books, skimming money off the top. It was so far from the truth that for a moment he couldn't speak.

'Don't *ever*,' he finally warned Leonidas in a low voice, 'make such a despicable insinuation again. I've given my life, my soul, to Marakaios Enterprises.'

Leonidas stared at him for a long moment, his jaw tight. 'You're not the only one,' he finally said, and walked out.

Antonios sank into his chair, his mind still spinning, and pulled his laptop towards him. Grimly he clicked the mouse to download his emails and refused to think about what Leonidas had just said.

A couple of hours later he heard voices in the reception area and lifted his head to see Lindsay coming through his door. A wave of relieved joy broke over him at the sight of her; she wore a floral sundress and her hair tumbled loose about her shoulders. She offered him a shy smile as she came in the room and Antonios rose from behind his desk, barely restraining himself from striding across the room and pulling her into a desperately needed embrace.

'I thought I'd see how you are,' she said with a little smile. 'And where you work. I hope you don't mind.'

'I don't.' Emotion bottled in his chest, making his voice sound abrupt. Lindsay frowned.

'Is everything all right, Antonios?'

'Fine. Everything's fine, now that you're here.' Her frown deepened at this but Antonios didn't care. He just needed to touch her. He came round from his desk and pulled her into his arms, fitting her against him, needing her there.

She pressed her hands to either side of his face, twisting to look up at him. 'You seem angry.'

'Just a little stressed. Nothing to worry about.' And to silence any further questions he kissed her, revelling in the honeyed sweetness of her mouth, the instant melting of her response.

He slid his hands down her body to cup her bottom and fit her even more snugly against his growing arousal. She let out a choked laugh.

'Antonios...'

'You know something I've never done in my office?'

'I think I can probably guess.'

He slid his hands under her sundress, fingers finding sweet, warm flesh. He rejoiced at the way she shuddered under his touch, her head falling onto his shoulder.

'Your PA is right outside…' she murmured, but offered no other resistance.

'The door is closed and incredibly soundproof.'

'How do you know?'

He didn't, but at this point he didn't care. 'Trust me,' he said, and hoisted her onto his desk. Lindsay's lovely eyes widened as he spread her legs and got rid of her underwear with one swift tug. They widened further when he stepped between her legs, stroking her softly as she moaned her response.

'This is crazy,' she murmured, and Antonios slid inside her.

'Crazy,' he agreed, 'and incredible.'

And Lindsay obviously agreed as her body arched under his and she wrapped her legs around his waist to pull him even more deeply inside her.

Afterwards he still didn't let her go, savouring the feel of her, already wanting her again. 'What do you think about going into Amfissa for lunch?' he asked.

Suddenly the thought of escaping the office, the entire estate, seemed like a wonderful and even necessary idea.

'Now?' She peered up at him again. 'But the party's tonight…'

'Right. Of course.' The hope that had seized him for a moment trickled away. He needed to stop by the villa, make sure the preparations were going well, check on his mother. His sisters would expect it. His family needed it.

Lindsay searched his face for a moment, a slight frown puckering her forehead. 'I suppose we could,' she said after a moment. 'For a few hours. I was just in the villa, trying to help your sisters. I think I'm more help to them by just staying out of the way.'

'They can be a bit officious when it comes

to party planning,' Antonios conceded with a smile, and Lindsay gave a rueful nod.

'Why don't we go?' she suggested softly. 'Have a date? They can do without us for an hour or two, surely.'

An hour or two snatched from a packed schedule. They'd had even less the last time they'd been together in Greece, Antonios acknowledged. Work had consumed him and he'd expected, wrongly, for Lindsay to simply slot herself into all that was going on around her.

He wouldn't make that mistake again.

'Let's go,' he said and, taking her by the hand, he led her out of the office.

Lindsay followed Antonios from the office, blinking in the bright sunlight. Ten minutes later they were in his SUV, speeding down the mountain towards Amfissa, the town no more than a cluster of red-roofed, whitewashed buildings huddled against the mountainside.

'I haven't even been in Amfissa before,' Lindsay said a bit ruefully, and Antonios shot her just as regretful a glance.

'I know. I was realizing again how little we actually did together before. That undoubtedly made things even harder for you.'

'Yes. You were busy, though, with work. I understood that.' At least, she'd tried to. But she knew her anxiety had been made worse by Antonios's absence, his total focus on work as soon as they'd returned to Greece.

Antonios flexed his hands on the steering wheel. 'I should have made time. We should have had a honeymoon.'

'Our meeting was our honeymoon,' Lindsay joked and Antonios shook his head.

'We'll have a proper honeymoon after my mother's party. When I can get away.'

'And when will that be, do you think?' Lindsay spoke lightly even as realization was slipping through her in an unwelcome rush. No matter what Antonios had said about things being different now, they surely couldn't be that different. He was still CEO of a company that demanded much of his time and energy. When she'd come into the office this morning he'd looked so grimly focused, so unhappy.

It had surprised and unsettled her, and it made her wonder if Antonios really could work less. If their marriage could work.

Plenty of women had workaholic husbands, she reminded herself. It didn't have to be a deal-breaker.

'Don't,' Antonios said softly, and reached over to link her hand with his.

She turned to him. 'Don't what?'

'Don't start worrying already. We'll make this work, Lindsay, I swear it. We both want it to work, don't we?'

'Yes—'

'Then it will.'

He sounded so confident, so sure, as sure as he had when he'd asked her out, when he'd asked her to marry him. She'd believed in him then, and she chose to believe in him now. At least for an afternoon when they could simply revel in each other's company, an afternoon out of time, out of reality.

And when you return to Villa Marakaios? When life catches up with you, with all of its expectations and demands?

She'd think about that later, Lindsay told herself, and pushed the questions to the furthest reaches of her mind. Today she just wanted to enjoy herself—and enjoy being with Antonios.

Once in Amfissa they strolled down the town's wide main boulevard, taking in the many different shops. Antonios was recognized by many of the townspeople and he stopped and spoke to them all, introducing Lindsay. She could handle small groups of people and everyone seemed so friendly, so interested, that the initial anxiety she felt melted away and she chatted with the different people easily, or as easily as she could considering they spoke different languages.

'Is it all right, meeting all these people?' Antonios asked as they walked away from a local joiner and his wife who had been shopping in the market, and had welcomed Lindsay with kisses on both of her cheeks.

'It's fine,' she answered, and meant it. 'I'm not anxious.' It was different, she realized, having Antonios by her side, concerned and supportive. Different when she didn't have the weight of expectation and potential disappointment on her. Not a magical cure by any means, and she knew she would still be dealing with her anxiety for years to come. But it was better. She felt stronger.

'Let's have some lunch,' Antonios said, and led her down a side street to a small taverna tucked away from prying eyes.

The inside of the restaurant was dim and quiet, with only a few patrons who barely looked up from their meals as they entered. Antonios spoke rapidly in Greek to the owner of the place, and within minutes he was ushering them to a private table at the back of the restaurant. The owner brought them menus, a bottle of spring water and two glasses before quietly disappearing.

'A little privacy never goes amiss,' Antonios said.

'I was fine,' Lindsay protested.

'I know you were. I was proud of you, Lindsay. But I want you to myself now.' He gave her a teasingly lascivious smile and she laughed and shook her head.

'You're insatiable.'

'Only when it comes to you.'

Which felt like some kind of miracle. She'd spent so much of her life feeling deficient and unworthy. Yet Antonios looked at her and saw someone strong, someone beautiful. Someone he loved.

'You know,' she said slowly, 'I think part of the reason I didn't tell you about my anxiety is because I didn't want you to look at me differently.' Antonios waited, eyebrows raised, clearly sensing she had more to say. 'When we met in New York you made me feel so special and beautiful and strong. And I was afraid you'd stop looking at me that way if you knew.'

'I wouldn't—'

'I know that now, Antonios, because you didn't. Because you know the truth and you still love me. You still make me feel special.' She blinked back tears of emotion as she reached for his hand. 'Even more special because you know me completely. I'm not hiding anything from you.'

He squeezed her hand. 'And I pray you never do or feel you have to.'

'I won't.'

They ordered then, and spent the next hour tasting each other's dishes and chatting companionably. Afterwards they strolled through the town, hand in hand as the cares fell away from them both.

Lindsay noticed how much more relaxed Antonios seemed, away from Villa Marakaios—or was it their renewed relationship that had smoothed away the lines of strain from his nose to his mouth and brought the sparkle back to his whisky-coloured eyes?

'I feel like I did back in New York,' she confessed as they sat on one of the stone walls that overlooked the valley, on one of the town's higher winding streets. 'When we first met.'

'That's a good thing, I hope?' Antonios answered, his eyebrows raised, and Lindsay smiled and nodded.

'Yes. Definitely. You seem more like you did in New York.'

'And how is that?'

'More relaxed. Happier.' She paused then asked cautiously, 'Sometimes it seems like work doesn't make you happy, Antonios. Like it's a huge strain.' She waited for him to say something in response but he didn't, just gazed out at the valley with his eyes narrowed.

'I suppose in New York I was free from the concerns of work and daily life,' he finally said, his gaze still on the view. 'It was, as you said before, a time apart.'

'So we need to figure out how to make things work amidst those concerns.'

'And we will,' Antonios said with the same confidence he'd shown in the restaurant. 'All that matters is that we love each other, Lindsay. The rest will work itself out.'

He raised her hand to his lips and kissed it, and Lindsay smiled and said nothing. She wanted to feel as confident as Antonios seemed to be, but worries still nagged at her, made her wonder just *how* things were going to work themselves out. Would Antonios work less? Would he entertain less? How were they actually going to manage the day-to-day of their joined lives?

A short while later they headed back to the car and drove in silence back to Villa Marakaios. Lindsay slid a sideways glance at Antonios as they approached the estate, silently noting how his eyes narrowed and his mouth hardened the moment they drove through the gates.

At their own villa he left her with a quick distracted kiss, telling her he needed to return to the office before the party that night. Reluctantly, Lindsay headed over to the main villa to see if she could help with the preparations. Antonios's sisters seemed to have affairs well in hand but she wanted to be seen to make an effort, even if she still found her relationship with her sisters-in-law to be one of tension and suspicion.

'Oh, Lindsay, where have you been? Was Antonios with you? Ava's been looking for him—'

'We went out for a bit,' Lindsay answered. 'Is everything all right?'

'Parthenope's been tied up all afternoon with Timon,' Xanthe explained. 'And Ava has decided she can't wear anything she owns and has gone shopping, of all things.' Xanthe rolled her eyes in exasperation.

'Is Timon all right?'

'Just a bit of cold,' Xanthe dismissed. 'But Parthenope was meant to deal with the caterers, where to have them set up, all of that. I've been busy myself with the decorations—'

'I could help,' Lindsay offered and Xanthe looked, perhaps rightly, sceptical. Lindsay straightened, threw back her shoulders. 'What do you need me to do?'

'Well…' Xanthe nibbled her lip. 'The housekeeper Maria is sorting them out in the kitchen, but she's in a flap because she wanted to do the cooking herself. Mama said no, because it was too much. Maria is not as young as she once was.'

'I see,' Lindsay said. 'So you want me to talk to Maria?'

Xanthe nodded in relief. 'Yes, and then show the caterers what to do.' Xanthe turned back to the table she was festooning with large silk bows, clearly itching to keep going with her own work. 'Do you think you could do that?' she tossed over her shoulder.

'Yes, of course,' Lindsay said with more confidence than she felt. She didn't even know where the kitchen was.

She watched Xanthe for a moment, fussing

with one of the bows, and then turned and made her uncertain way to the kitchen, opening a few random doors until one of the house staff pointed her towards the large, light room at the back of the house.

The caterers were bringing in large plastic-wrapped trays of hors d'oeuvres, watched over by a silent and surly Maria. Lindsay had seen the housekeeper in passing and had probably been introduced to her on that first awful day, but they'd never had a conversation.

She took a deep breath and approached her. '*Herete*, Maria,' she said as cheerfully as she could. 'Is everything all right?'

Maria just looked at her blankly, and Lindsay realized the older woman did not speak English. And she, unfortunately, had no more than a few words of Greek.

She gestured to the caterers and raised her eyebrows in query, asking haltingly, *'Ti kanete?'* How are you?

In answer Maria let out a torrent of Greek that Lindsay could not begin to understand, but she certainly got the gist of Maria's bitterness at having strangers invade her kitchen. Making soothing noises, she led the woman over to the table in a sunny alcove, and listened with all signs of interest and attention as Maria continued to lament in a language she didn't speak.

Fifteen minutes later, having vented her spleen, Maria seemed somewhat appeased, and with gestures and an absurd amount of miming Lindsay suggested she organize the hors d'oeuvres. The caterers could have a respite from Maria scowling at them, and the housekeeper would hopefully feel she was being consulted.

Twenty minutes later things were going smoothly, and Lindsay felt rather ridiculously proud of herself for coping with it all. She was smiling as she came back to the front house, stopping when she saw Antonios come through the door of the living room, scowling.

'Is everything all right?' she asked, and Antonios jerked his gaze towards her, his face clearing, Lindsay suspected, by sheer force of will.

'Fine. Are things in hand in the kitchen? I just got an earful from Xanthe.'

'Yes, I think so. I was just down with Maria.'

'Were you?' Antonios's eyebrows rose at that, and Lindsay smiled self-consciously.

'I didn't realize she didn't speak English, but we managed all right.'

'That's very good to hear.'

'Shall we go back to the villa?' she asked, and Antonios nodded. Lindsay could still see lines of tension bracketing his mouth and eyes and she stopped in front of him, reaching up to cup his cheek. 'Are you sure you're all right?' she asked quietly.

Antonios closed his eyes briefly, seeming to take strength from her small caress. 'I'm fine,' he said, and Lindsay heard the note of implacability enter his voice. He sounded, she thought, like she used to, claiming things were fine when they clearly weren't.

As she followed Antonios out of the villa, she wondered if he would be as honest with her as she had learned to be with him, and tell her what was going on.

CHAPTER TEN

ANTONIOS STOOD ON the edge of the living room, watching as guests chatted and circulated amidst the staff holding trays of hors d'oeuvres. His mother sat on a chair in the centre of the room, looking weary and yet happy as she held court over all the family, friends and neighbours that had been invited to her name day party.

His gaze moved to the opposite corner of the room where Lindsay stood, looking pale and lovely and amazingly poised, chatting with a guest, a smile making her seem radiant. She was, Antonios thought, the most beautiful and elegant woman in the room.

While they were getting ready, back at their own villa, he'd assured her that she wouldn't need to be the centre of attention and could leave if she felt uncomfortable. Invariably, though, Lindsay attracted attention. She was beautiful, and she was his wife. People wanted to meet her, talk to her, and Antonios had responsibilities of his own. As much as he wanted to, he couldn't hide in the corner, protecting his wife.

Not, he acknowledged with a small wry smile, that Lindsay needed protecting. She'd been more than holding her own so far tonight, chatting with people as they approached her, smiling and laughing. Pride surged through him, mixed with love. She was everything he'd ever wanted in a wife, a partner.

His gaze narrowed as he watched Leonidas come up to her. He still hadn't agreed to give Leonidas access to any of the company's financial information, and he didn't think he ever could, not without betraying his father.

He'd thought, more than once, about telling Leonidas the truth. Sharing the burden. But it wasn't his secret to share. He'd made a promise. A vow. If he couldn't honour it, what sort of man was he?

One whose family is being torn apart by secrecy.

Now, as he watched Leonidas talk to Lindsay,

he wondered if his brother intended to put pressure on his wife. Leonidas was so angry and bitter that Antonios wouldn't put such an underhand tactic past him at this point.

Lindsay frowned at Leonidas and every protective instinct in Antonios reared up. The last thing he needed or wanted was his brother breathing his bitter poison into his wife's ear. His mouth set in a grim line, he headed towards his brother and his wife.

Lindsay had been trying to answer Leonidas's questions in a relaxed manner but the more he talked, the harder it was to ignore the edge to his voice.

Are you happy to be back at Villa Marakaios? It's all marital bliss, is it? You and Antonios have everything you want, I suppose? He certainly does.

Lindsay couldn't tell if Leonidas knew the truth of their earlier troubles or if he was simply bitter about what he perceived as his brother's good fortune. What was coming through, loud and clear, was the resentment and animosity he felt towards Antonios.

'Everything all right here?' Antonios asked as he strolled up to them. His voice was pleasant but his gaze had snapped to Lindsay, and she could see the question in his eyes.

'Fine,' Leonidas answered for both of them. 'Just getting to know my sister-in-law. Wondering what she sees in you.' Lindsay thought Leonidas had meant this as a joke, but it fell rather flat.

'I wonder myself every day,' Antonios answered, his voice light but his face unsmiling. 'Lindsay, there are some people who would like to meet you. The Atrikes family. They're local business owners. Why don't you come with me?' He held out his hand and, with a moment's hesitant glance at Leonidas, whose expression had ironed out to bland boredom, she took it.

'What's going on between you and Leonidas?' she asked when they were alone in a private alcove off the library.

'What do you mean?'

'You clearly don't get along,' Lindsay said bluntly. 'And yet you work together.'

Antonios twitched his shoulders in an impatient shrug. 'Nothing more than a little brotherly competition.'

'Over what?' He just shrugged again, not answering, and frustration fired through her. 'Antonios, can't you tell me? You didn't like it when you were in the dark about how I was feeling, but now you're the same—'

'It's just a business matter—' he cut her off, his tone dismissive '—it will sort itself out.'

'What kind of business matter?'

'Nothing you need to concern yourself about.' He'd kept his voice mild but Lindsay still felt the rebuke. Nothing he wanted to concern her with, he'd meant.

'You're doing so well tonight, Lindsay,' he continued, and dropped a kiss onto her forehead. 'You're the most beautiful woman in the room, the most elegant and poised. I'm proud of you.'

She smiled and turned her face so he could kiss her on the mouth. He did so, lingeringly, and Lindsay knew both of them were thinking about later that evening, after the party, when they could be alone.

'I'm proud of you, Antonios,' she told him. 'You've led your family and your business so well in the absence of your father. So many people have been telling me how you've taken the helm of Marakaios Enterprises without a single misstep.'

Antonios smiled at this, but it was a small, tight smile that didn't reach his eyes.

'We should go. The Atrikes family are waiting.'

A little while later they headed back to the living area, where Xanthe and Parthenope were ushering people towards the dining room, where platters of food were laid out.

Daphne rose from her chair, her hands outstretched towards Antonios. 'Antonios, Lindsay. Come celebrate with me.'

Lindsay came forward and took Daphne's hand, feeling how fragile it was in hers, the skin papery, the bones seeming hollow, like a bird's.

Daphne smiled wryly, as if she noticed Lindsay's awareness, and squeezed her hand. 'Tonight is for happiness,' she said quietly, and her gaze moved to Antonios. 'Yes?'

'Yes,' Lindsay said firmly and gently squeezed her mother-in-law's hand back.

The party lasted until well after midnight, even though Daphne excused herself earlier, tired as she was. By the time she and Antonios returned to their little villa, Lindsay was exhausted, her feet aching.

'I think it was a success,' she said as she kicked off her heels with a sigh of relief. She hadn't had a single moment of true anxiety, at least in part because Antonios had been aware of when she needed to take a step back, have a moment's space and peace.

'I think so,' Antonios agreed. He shrugged out of his suit jacket and undid the knot of his tie. Even though he'd been his charming, confident self throughout the whole evening, Lindsay had sensed his restlessness and tension and it felt like a thorn in her side, in their marriage.

'Are you sure everything is all right, Antonios?' she asked. 'Between you and Leonidas?'

'It's fine,' he dismissed and took her into his

arms. 'And the last thing I want to talk or even think about now is my brother. Do you know how beautiful you look in that dress?'

Lindsay glanced down at the pale blue evening gown she wore, the silk rippling in a shimmering sheet to the floor, reminding her of water. She'd never cared much about clothes one way or the other, but she loved the look on Antonios's face when he saw her in something beautiful. When he so clearly thought *she* was beautiful.

'You look gorgeous,' Antonios said in a growl as he pulled her to him. 'But I couldn't stop thinking about peeling it off you all evening.'

Lindsay laughed softly, already breathless with anticipation. 'And will you make that a reality, do you think?'

'I intend to right now.' His gaze blazed into hers as he reached around to her back and slowly, sensuously, tugged the zip all the way down to her hips. The dress fell from her shoulders and, with one tiny shrug, it slid down to her waist.

The style had precluded the wearing of a bra and Lindsay wasn't so generously endowed that she needed one, so now she stood before him, completely bare to the waist, basking in the admiration, the *adoration* she saw in his eyes.

A lump of emotion rose in her throat and Antonios tugged her towards him by the hand. 'What are you thinking?' he asked hoarsely. 'You look as if you're about to cry.'

'I was wondering how I ever could have left you,' Lindsay whispered, her voice catching. 'Even for a moment.'

He pulled her towards him, her breasts colliding with the crisp cotton of his shirt, the friction sending shivery arrows of pleasure ricocheting through her. 'Never again,' Antonios whispered against her hair as he slid his hands up her bare back to cradle her face. 'Never leave me again, Lindsay. Promise. I couldn't bear it.'

'I promise,' she whispered, and then lost herself to Antonios's passionate, desperate kiss.

The next few weeks seemed to pass in a golden blur of contentment and joy: days spent working on her research or walking through the countryside, taking the first steps in getting to know Antonios's family. His sisters were still a little guarded, but they'd thawed when Lindsay had, at Antonios's urging, explained about her anxiety.

Parthenope's face had fallen and she'd pulled Lindsay into a spontaneous hug. 'You should have told us. It would have made such a difference.'

'Parthenope thought you were a snob,' Ava confided and Parthenope pulled away from Lindsay, blushing.

'Ava!'

'Because you're so smart,' Ava continued, shooting her sister a mischievous glance. 'She's jealous, really. I'm the only one who went to university.'

'I got married instead,' Parthenope said, her cheeks bright red.

'I'm not sure a doctorate in number theory is something to be jealous of,' Lindsay said wryly. Her mind reeled from her sisters-in-law's admissions. 'It's not very useful.'

'Antonios told us it was,' Xanthe piped up. 'He said it would help with all sorts of advancements in technology and science.'

'Well, maybe,' Lindsay allowed. The thought

that Antonios had championed her research sent a tingling warmth through her.

'We did wonder if you thought you were too good for us,' Parthenope admitted, her face still flushed, and Lindsay's jaw nearly dropped.

'I never thought that,' she said. 'Not once.'

They all smiled at each other, awkwardly and yet with affection, and while Lindsay knew she might not have been what Antonios's sisters had been expecting or even wanting for his wife, she knew they accepted her. A few weeks ago their acceptance would have made her feel guilty, wondering yet again if she should have been honest about her issues when she'd been in Greece before. Now she recognized that she couldn't have been, that both she and Antonios were different people now, capable of different things.

A week after Daphne's birthday party Antonios had asked her if they could move into the main villa. 'My mother would like us there,' he said. 'And I would like to be there. We'll have our own wing, and you can redecorate as you like—'

His thoughtfulness nearly brought tears to her eyes. 'Of course we can move back to the main villa,' she said.

Yet it was a little strange to be back in the house where she'd once been so unhappy. She walked down the upstairs corridor, her footsteps muffled on the thick carpet, and remembered how she'd run up these stairs, spots dancing before her eyes, everything in her aching, as she'd excused herself from yet another endless social function, Antonios so wilfully oblivious.

In the huge sumptuous bathroom she remembered how she'd locked the door and curled up against the marble tub, hugging her knees to her chest and rocking back and forth as she'd tried to calm her racing heart.

And in the bedroom she remembered how Antonios had brought her such incredible pleasure, and how she'd left him one chilly morning, the grey light of dawn filtering through the curtains as she'd kissed him goodbye and felt her heart break.

So many memories, and she didn't want to linger on them for too long. She wanted to make new memories, have new dreams. Inadvertently, Lindsay pressed her hand against her stomach. They hadn't used protection in the last few weeks, something that made her insides lurch with both excitement and alarm. She knew Antonios had wanted to start a family right away; she'd been more cautious. But now she thought about a baby—Antonios's baby—and a smile spread across her face at the possibility.

Antonios came into the bedroom, resting his hands on her shoulders as he stood behind her. Both of them were silent, gazing at the wide bed with its cream silk duvet, the shutters of the windows open to the view of the mountains.

Lindsay knew they were both remembering, reliving those last moments. Her final farewell. Then Antonios brushed a kiss against the nape of her neck and it felt like a benediction. They were both moving on from the past.

'I have something to show you,' he said, his breath fanning her skin and making her shiver.

'You do?'

'Come.' He tugged her by the hand down the corridor of their private wing, towards a room

Lindsay hadn't been in before. He pushed open the door and then stepped aside so she could enter.

Her breath caught in her chest as she took in the spacious sunlit room: the wide oak desk with the top-of-the-line desktop computer, the comfortable chair, the bookshelves and the huge dry-erase board, just like she'd had in her office back in New York.

'For your research,' he said simply. 'If there's anything else you need, just let me know and I'll get it for you.'

She turned and threw her arms around his neck. 'There's nothing else I need,' she told him as she kissed him. 'Nothing else at all.'

Another week slid by, a week blurred by pleasure and love, and yet not without its moments of disquiet. Antonios still spent all his days and many of his evenings at work, and Lindsay couldn't ignore the strain that etched lines on his face and made him quiet and irritable whenever she asked him about it.

Love was complicated, she reminded herself. *Life* was. Whatever Antonios was dealing with, he'd tell her in his own time. They could deal with it.

But one night she woke up to an empty bed and, with unease crawling along her spine, she rose and went to their adjoining living area, stopping in the doorway when she saw Antonios standing by the window, one hand braced against the glass.

'Antonios…'

He didn't turn at the sound of her voice. 'I couldn't sleep,' he said, his voice flat and toneless.

'Is everything all right?' she asked. It was the same question she'd asked before, over and over, and as usual Antonios gave the same answer.

'It's fine.'

'Something's going on, Antonios,' Lindsay protested. 'I can feel it. You're unhappy—'

'Just a little stressed,' he corrected, but Lindsay felt it was more than that, deeper than that.

She also knew she wouldn't get any answers from Antonios now. Wordlessly, she went back to bed, lay flat on her back and stared up at the ceiling.

Why wouldn't Antonios tell her what was going on? He'd been hurt that she'd kept so much from him, and he'd never ever noticed she was unhappy. Yet now she was noticing and Antonios didn't seem to want her to.

Sighing, Lindsay told herself yet again to be patient. To trust. They could get through this. She had to believe that.

A month after Daphne's name day party Lindsay received an email from a university in New York City, offering her an assistant professorship of Pure Mathematics. She stared at it in surprise, knowing she shouldn't be so shocked since her supervisor had hinted that her research was being well received by academia in general. But that had been a lifetime ago, when she'd only had her research to think about, to keep her company…

And now? She felt a treacherous flicker of doubt and yearning. She loved being with Antonios, was enjoying this time in Greece…*but for the rest of her life?*

She looked up from her computer and gazed

unseeingly out at the pine-covered mountains. She and Antonios had been enjoying a honeymoon period to their marriage, she realized. But even the honeymoon had its bumps, with Antonios's stress over work. And when that phase wore off, when he worked even harder, when the stress and strain of that work took an even greater toll?

Antonios had made it clear he couldn't leave Greece. But what if he needed to? What if working for Marakaios Enterprises, for whatever reason he refused to name, was killing him, destroying his happiness?

What if he needed something different as much as she did—or even more?

The thought was so incredible, so revolutionary, that Lindsay couldn't take it in fully. And maybe it was just wishful thinking because she wanted Antonios's plans to fit in with her own. But she'd tied herself to him and promised to try life in Greece again. She couldn't suggest something else now, not even for his sake. Antonios wouldn't countenance it for a moment.

And, really, she couldn't imagine Antonios

anywhere else. This was his home, his kingdom. Yet she also knew she missed the excitement of teaching a class, discussing number theory with students and professors. Being part of a community, however small, of people who were as passionate and excited about mathematics as she was.

Restless and more than a little anxious, Lindsay closed her laptop and headed outside. It was a glorious fall day and the estate gardens were still in full flower. She walked down the winding brick paths that led to different gardens: the walled herb garden where she'd talked to Daphne, the courtyard with the fountain where she and Antonios had reconciled and made love. Just looking at the stone lip of the fountain where she'd wrapped herself around his body made her blush and smile.

She sank onto a stone bench, staring at that fountain, trying to untangle all the feelings that had become twisted up inside her. Hope and fear. Frustration and joy. Anxiety—not for herself, but for Antonios.

'Li-li!' Lindsay turned around to see two-year-old Timon toddling towards her. He'd started calling her Li-li a few days ago, much to everyone's amusement. Now Lindsay reached out and grabbed him by his chubby hands.

'Have you escaped, young man?' she asked, and Timon grinned up at her uncomprehendingly; he was learning both English and Greek, but he understood Greek much better.

'Timon!' Parthenope appeared around the corner, worry replaced by exasperation as she caught sight of her son. She let out a stream of scolding Greek but the little boy just giggled. Rolling her eyes at Lindsay, Parthenope gathered her son up on her lap and sat next to her on the bench.

'You are well?' she asked, a frown settling between her straight brows, and Lindsay laughed lightly.

'Do I not look well?'

'You look worried.' She hesitated then asked cautiously, 'Are things all right between you and Antonios?'

Lindsay stiffened at the implication that Parthenope, and who knew who else, suspected they weren't. 'Yes, of course.'

'Because, you know, when you left for New York he walked around like a raging lion. He pretended he was fine; he wouldn't tell us a thing, but we all knew better.'

Lindsay fought a flush as Parthenope subjected her to a searching gaze. 'Well…things are a lot better than that,' she said after a moment. 'We're working out our problems.'

At least, she hoped they were.

Parthenope laid a hand on her arm as Timon squirmed out of her lap. 'Marriage is not always easy.'

'No, that's what your mother said,' Lindsay said with a small smile. '"Endlessly complicated and difficult" were her exact words.'

Parthenope let out a little laugh. 'Perhaps not quite that bad. But if you both try, it will be good, yes?'

Lindsay saw the hope and concern in Parthenope's eyes and slowly nodded. She sincerely hoped trying was enough. But was Antonios even trying? If he was, surely he would share some of his concerns with her. Maybe, Lindsay thought, she needed to ask him more bluntly. Demand, even, out of her love for him.

She smiled at Parthenope, not wanting to burden her sister-in-law with her private concerns. 'Yes,' she said, 'it will be good.'

That night Antonios stayed late at work, which left Lindsay alone in their bedroom, waiting for him and thinking far too much. At nearly eleven o'clock at night she finally broke down and headed out into the night to look for him.

The air was cool and crisp and she shivered in just her light sweater and jeans as she walked down the deserted drives towards the office building; she could see a single light burning inside.

The front door was open and she slipped silently inside, her heart starting to beat hard. She walked towards Antonios's office; his door was ajar and she stood at the threshold, peeked inside.

At the sight of him her heart lurched with fear, swooped with sorrow. He looked so despairing, his head cradled in his hands, his shoulders bowed.

'Antonios…' she whispered and he jerked up straight, anger blazing in his eyes.

'What are you doing here?'

'I was looking for you.'

'You shouldn't have. You knew I was working.'

She knew his anger was a defence mechanism but it still stung. 'It's nearly midnight, Antonios.'

'I have a lot going on at the moment.'

She took a step into the room, glanced at the computer screen that had been left up, with its many columns of numbers. 'What are you doing?'

He slammed down the lid of his laptop. 'Don't. Don't look at that.'

Lindsay felt herself go cold at the implacable note in his voice. 'Why not?' she asked as reasonably as she could. 'It's only numbers.'

'And you're so good at numbers,' Antonios shot back.

Lindsay jerked back at the sneer in his voice. 'Antonios, what is going on? Why are you acting this way, hiding—'

'I'm not hiding,' he returned in a near roar. '*Theos*, Lindsay, just let me be.' He rose from his chair, pacing the room like a caged lion, one hand clenching in his hair. He looked, Lindsay thought, like a man in torment.

'I don't understand what's going on,' she said quietly. 'And I think I need to.'

Antonios didn't even turn around. 'Trust me, you don't.'

'Does this have to do with Leonidas?' Antonios didn't answer and, filled with frustration, Lindsay walked up to him, put her hands on his taut back. 'Damn it, Antonios, stop hiding things from me. You're making a double standard for our marriage and it's not fair.'

'Don't talk to me about what's fair,' Antonios answered bleakly, and she shook her head.

'I don't understand.'

'I don't want you to understand.' He turned around, clasping her cold hands in his. 'Lindsay, you're right. I am hiding something from you, but I have to.' Anguish lit his eyes and twisted his features. 'Please believe me. This has nothing to do with you, with us. It's just business.

Naturally, there are some confidential matters I can't discuss—'

'Confidential matters that are tearing you apart, making you look haunted?' Lindsay finished. 'Making you seem like someone else entirely. Antonios, you're wrong. This has everything to do with us.' She stared at him, watched as his mouth thinned and his eyes hardened. She knew he wouldn't tell her anything now.

Wordlessly, she slipped her hands from his and walked from the room.

CHAPTER ELEVEN

ANTONIOS LISTENED TO the front door of the office close and with a groan he sank back in his chair, raking his hands through his hair. *Theos*, what had he been about to do?

He flipped up the screen of the laptop and watched as the financial figures of Marakaios Enterprises filled the screen. Figures he'd been contemplating doctoring to hide his father's shame—and add to his own. He couldn't believe he'd been contemplating doing something illegal for his father, or at least his father's memory. His father had done his fair share of tinkering with numbers, and Antonios had felt nothing but a sickening disdain. Yet now he'd been about to do the same thing.

He rose from his chair and restlessly paced the length of his office. He felt a need to escape not just the confines of the room, but of his life.

Of the promise he'd made to his father, and the shackle Marakaios Enterprises had become to him.

He'd alienated his brother by hiding the truth of his father's actions, and now he'd done the same to Lindsay. He groaned aloud, shaking his head. Somehow this had to stop before it was too late. But maybe it was too late already.

A little after two in the morning Antonios headed back to the villa. Lindsay was already asleep, curled on her side, her knees tucked up to her chest like a child's. Antonios doubted he'd be able to sleep. It had eluded him most nights these last few weeks. Leonidas was barely talking to him, and the tension in the office was palpable, not just to him but to all the staff. And he still didn't know what to do.

He was still staring gritty-eyed at the ceiling when, an hour later, a light yet urgent tapping at the door of the bedroom had every sense springing to alert. Antonios rose from the bed, careful not to disturb Lindsay, and went to answer the door.

'Xanthe—'

'Antonios, it's Mama.' His sister's face was pale and pinched, tears shining in her eyes. Antonios felt as if his heart had stilled for a moment before beginning to thud with hard, painful beats.

'What has happened?'

'She woke up in the night, moaning and in pain. Maria has called the doctor. But she seems…it seems…' Xanthe couldn't go on, tears spilling down her cheeks, and Antonios hugged her briefly, murmuring meaningless words of consolation before he strode down the corridor.

His mother's room was lit only by a bedside lamp and its pale glow threw her features into shocking relief. Antonios knew his mother had been getting more tired and frail in the last few weeks, but the reality of it and her illness hit him now with painful force. The skin of her face was drawn tightly over her bones and she lay back on the pillows, her eyes closed, her breathing shallow.

Swallowing hard, Antonios approached the bed and perched carefully on its edge. '*Yeia sou*, Mama,' he said softly.

Daphne's eyelids fluttered but that was all. Antonios felt a swooping sensation in his chest, like missing a step. He reached for her hand, noticing how thin her wrist had become, her fingers claw-like. He didn't know what to say; everything felt like a platitude or a lie, so he just held her hand.

After a few minutes the doctor arrived and Antonios stood up, watching as the man checked his mother over, took her pulse and blood pressure.

'Well?' he bit out when he could stand it no longer.

Spiros Tallos straightened slowly and turned to face him. The older man had been the family doctor for two generations; he had set Antonios's leg when he'd broken it, falling out of a tree when he was six.

'She's dying, Antonios,' Spiro said gently. 'But we all knew that.'

'She has not been like this before,' Antonios answered, his voice terse.

'She is closer to the end.'

Everything in him roared in denial. 'How long?'

'It is impossible to say.'

'Guess,' Antonios snapped, and Spiros sighed sadly.

'It could be days, or it could be weeks. There will be good days and bad days, but continued decline.' He gave a little shrug, spreading his hands. 'I am sorry.'

Antonios turned away so the doctor would not see the naked grief on his face; he felt the burn of tears behind his lids and blinked them away rapidly. 'Thank you,' he finally said, when he trusted himself to speak. He cleared his throat. 'Can you…is there anything you can give her, for pain relief?'

'Of course,' Spiros said, and turned back to Daphne. Antonios turned to Xanthe, who was crying quietly. Wordlessly, he drew her into a hug and Xanthe took a shuddering breath, her cheek pressed against her shoulder.

'I know it shouldn't be a shock,' she whispered haltingly, 'but it is.'

Yes, it was. A terrible shock, a grim reality.

Antonios closed his eyes, wished Lindsay were here with him. He longed for her quiet, comforting presence, the steadiness and strength he'd always appreciated in her. And yet he didn't want to have to tell her how Daphne had declined.

'Antonios.'

Xanthe jerked out of his arms and he hurried to his mother's bedside. 'Mama…'

'I want…' Daphne swallowed convulsively, her breath coming in shudders and gasps. Xanthe pressed a fist to her lips and Antonios took his mother's hand.

'Don't speak, it's too much for you now—'

She shook her head, the movement violent. 'I want….Leonidas,' she finally managed.

'I'll get him,' Xanthe offered and Antonios nodded his thanks.

Ten taut minutes later Leonidas was striding into the room, his hair dishevelled, his shirt untucked from the jeans he'd hastily put on before coming from his own villa to here.

His gaze snapped to Antonios and then back to his mother and, without a word of greeting for his brother, he sat on the opposite side of the bed and took his mother's other hand.

'Mama.'

Antonios began to rise. 'I'll go,' he murmured. 'You can have privacy…'

Daphne shook her head again. 'No. The two of you here. That is what I want. Together.' Neither Antonios nor Leonidas spoke and with effort Daphne drew her hands together so their hands, clasped in hers, were touching.

'There is too much pain and bitterness between you,' she said, her words coming slowly, her breathing laboured. 'You must make peace with each other now, before it is too late.' A tear snaked its way down her withered cheek. 'Before I am gone.'

Leonidas's hand twitched against Antonios's. They were both, he suspected, itching to pull their hands away, yet they wouldn't for the sake of their mother.

'We're fine, Mama,' Leonidas said placatingly, and Antonios's mouth tightened. *Fine*. He was beginning to hate that word. They were not fine.

Lindsay had not been fine. In that moment, nothing, about anything, felt *fine*.

Daphne must have agreed for she shook her head, her hands tightening on her sons'. 'No,' she rasped. 'You have been angry and bitter with Antonios for too many years, Leonidas. It must stop now.'

Years? Antonios blinked, shooting his brother a sideways glance. Leonidas's jaw was tight but he said nothing.

'Don't worry about Antonios and me,' Leonidas finally bit out and Daphne let out a soft cry that tore at Antonios's heart.

'Of course I worry about you,' she answered, her voice choking. 'I know what Evangelos has cost both of you…'

Antonios's whole body tensed and he strove to keep his voice even as he asked, 'What do you mean, Mama?'

She turned her anguished face towards him. 'Making you the CEO—'

'You think he shouldn't have?' The words were out before Antonios could think better of them.

'Oh, Antonios, it doesn't matter what I think,' Daphne said, the words so soft Antonios had to lean forward to hear them. 'What matters is what it has done to you—'

'Done to me—'

'And Leonidas.'

Antonios simply sat and stared, his mind spinning. At least, he thought numbly, his mother hadn't known about his father's debt. For a moment, he'd been afraid she had.

'You must reconcile,' Daphne insisted. 'And be at peace with one another.'

'I—' Antonios began, but Leonidas cut across him.

'We will reconcile, Mama,' he said. 'We will be as brothers should be.'

This seemed to be exactly the right thing to say, for a beatific smile transformed Daphne's tired face and then she sank back against the pillows and closed her eyes. Just seconds later she was asleep.

Antonios and Leonidas remained on either side of her for a moment until, by silent, tense agreement, they rose and retreated to the far side of the room.

'What did the doctor say?' Leonidas asked.

'He said she would continue to decline. It could be days or weeks.'

'But not months.'

'No.'

They were both silent and, despite Leonidas's promise to their mother, neither of them, Antonios noted, was making any attempt to reconcile. Damn it, he hadn't even realized they'd needed to reconcile, at least not before the whole thing with Adair Hotels had blown up.

Leonidas glanced at their mother, lying asleep in bed. She looked peaceful, despite the agitation she'd shown them both just moments ago.

'Someone should stay with her,' he said.

'I will,' Antonios answered. Leonidas gave him one long, considering look and then nodded. 'Fine. Wake me if…if anything changes.'

Antonios nodded and Leonidas left. He turned back to Daphne, feeling weary in body and soul. Knowing he would not sleep that night, he pulled a chair up to the side of the bed and sat down.

Antonios wasn't in bed when Lindsay woke before dawn. Normally she wouldn't have woken up properly, but the cool expanse of sheet she encountered when she stretched her legs made her whole body jolt with shock.

Then she remembered their argument last night and her heart sank. Had he stayed in the office all night? And how were they going to get past this?

Too awake now even to consider going back to bed, Lindsay paced the elegant confines of the bedroom for a while before curling up in a chair by the window and watching the sun's first pearly rays peek over the mountains, touching the dense forest of pine trees with gold. She wondered where her husband was.

At half past eight the door to the bedroom finally opened and Lindsay sprang from her chair.

'Where were you?' she demanded, her voice coming out in a harpy's shriek.

Antonios looked at her wearily, his face haggard, his eyes shadowed. 'Daphne,' he said simply, and all of Lindsay's petty concerns faded in light of this far greater worry.

'What happened—is she all right?'

Antonios shook his head. 'I need a shower,'

he said and, without another word for Lindsay, he disappeared into the bathroom, closing the door behind him.

Lindsay paced the bedroom once more, fresh anxiety eating away at her. She feared for Daphne, for Antonios, who would feel the loss of his mother so keenly, and for their marriage, which suddenly seemed a fragile and untested thing, its foundation rocked by every silence, each argument.

Ten minutes later Antonios came out of the shower, his hair damp and spiky, a towel slung low around his hips. Lindsay stood up from where she'd sunk onto the bed and stared at him, her heart starting to pound.

Wordlessly, Antonios strode towards her and then pulled her, suddenly and urgently, into a tight embrace, his face buried in her neck. Lindsay put her arms around him, hugging him back just as tightly. Neither of them spoke for a long moment, just absorbed each other's uncertainty and pain. This was all the reassurance she needed, she told herself, that Antonios loved her. They would weather these storms.

Finally Antonios eased back, his face bleak. 'It won't be long.'

A lump formed in Lindsay's throat and she blinked back tears. 'Oh, Antonios, I'm sorry.' He nodded, and she sniffed. 'I don't know why it feels sudden—'

'Death is always a shock.' He rubbed his face, clearly exhausted from his night spent in Daphne's room. 'I'm sure she'd like a visit from you.'

'Of course,' Lindsay answered quickly. 'Is she…is she lucid?'

'At times. She spoke, for a little while, to me and Leonidas.' Antonios's mouth hardened at that and his gaze flicked away.

'What did she say?' Lindsay asked quietly, and Antonios shook his head.

'It doesn't matter.'

Lindsay didn't answer because whatever Daphne had said to her two sons was personal, private, and yet…it did matter. Of that she was sure. It was just one more thing Antonios didn't want to tell her. Anxiety churned inside her and Antonios turned away.

'I should get to the office.'

'You haven't even slept—'

'There are things to be done.'

'And what about you and Leonidas?' she blurted.

Antonios swung back towards her, his gaze narrowed. 'What about us?'

Lindsay took a deep breath. 'Antonios, I know you're keeping something from me. Something that is hurting you. I kept something from you, and when I told you it was such a relief. Won't you tell me?'

His face contorted briefly and then he shook his head. 'No. I'm sorry, Lindsay, but I can't. Not…' He took a breath, let it out slowly. 'I can tell you that Leonidas is angry with me, and has been for years.'

'Why?'

'Because our father appointed me CEO. Because I have the authority he wants.' He let out a weary sigh. 'Our mother wants us to reconcile.'

'And have you?' Lindsay asked quietly. Antonios shook his head.

'No, Leonidas left after Mama was settled.

And I'm not sure Leonidas and I will ever see eye to eye.'

'And will we?' Lindsay asked softly.

Antonios frowned. 'I told you before. This doesn't affect our marriage.'

'Of course it does,' Lindsay cried. 'All of it does. You think the tension and anger I see in you every day, the bitterness between you and your brother, doesn't affect us?'

Antonios folded his arms, his expression implacable. 'I can't tell Leonidas.'

'Why not?'

'Because I made a promise to my father.'

Lindsay stared at him searchingly, wishing she knew what to say, how to reach across this impasse. Perhaps now, with his mother so near death, was not the time to push.

Slowly she nodded, swallowing hard. 'All right.'

Antonios's expression softened and he pulled her into a hug. 'Thank you for understanding,' he said softly, pressing a kiss against her hair, and Lindsay closed her eyes. She was afraid her understanding wouldn't be enough…for either of them.

* * *

Daphne died three days later. Lindsay had been to see her several times, sitting by her bed and talking to her even though Daphne slipped in and out of lucidity. Xanthe, Parthenope and Ava came, too, brushing their mother's thin white hair, holding her hand, singing songs from their childhood.

The process of saying farewell, Lindsay thought, was so important. She'd missed it with her own mother, who had left and never returned, never reached out even once. It had been as if she'd died, or perhaps even worse.

This slow goodbye was painful but necessary, for her as well as for Antonios and his family.

And yet even as the end loomed nearer, and Daphne slipped deeper and deeper into unconsciousness, death was, as Antonios had said, a shock.

Lindsay was in her study, trying and failing to focus on the research she'd ignored for days, when Antonios came to tell her. She'd pulled up the email from the university and had drafted the first stilted sentences of a reply:

Thank you very much for your email. I have greatly enjoyed my time in the Mathematics Department and am honoured to…

To what? …have been asked? …accept? Her mind churned with possibilities, fears and desires.

'Lindsay.'

She turned from her laptop, her heart lurching into her throat at the bleak and haggard look on Antonios's face.

'Not—'

'Yes.' His mouth compressed and he took a quick steadying breath. 'I was there. So was Parthenope.'

'And the others?'

He shook his head. 'We've been taking it in turns to sit with her.'

'Oh, Antonios.' She rose from her desk and put her arms around him. Antonios pulled her to him as he had before, fitting her body to his. 'I'm so sorry.'

'I know.'

They remained in a silent embrace, needing

no words. Then Antonios eased back. 'I'll need to start making arrangements for the funeral.'

'Of course. If there is anything I can do—'

He shook his head and left. Lindsay glanced back at her laptop.

Thank you for your email. I am honoured to...

With a sigh, she closed the laptop and went to find Antonios's sisters.

The funeral was two days later, at the Orthodox church in Amfissa, with a large crowd of townspeople along with all of the family, staff and employees of Marakaios Enterprises. Lindsay saw how Antonios and Leonidas stood apart from each other, their sisters like a barrier between them, as the coffin was lowered into the hard, stony earth.

There was a sombre reception back at the house, painfully reminiscent of Daphne's name day party, yet without her holding court in the centre of the room.

Lindsay helped organize things in the kitchen, glad to be out of the spotlight and knowing Antonios and his siblings needed time together. Her husband, she saw, was still not talking to Leonidas, never mind attempting some kind of reconciliation.

By the end of the day she was exhausted and aching in body and spirit, grateful to retreat up to their private wing. She hadn't seen Antonios for the last hour and had assumed he was closeted somewhere with his siblings.

He opened the door to their bedroom before her hand had touched the knob, causing her to give a small gasp of surprise.

'I didn't realize you'd come up—'

'Yet here I am.' Antonios's voice was clipped, his expression grim. Lindsay closed the door behind her.

'Is everything…' she began, only to have Antonios fill in unpleasantly,

'All right? No, Lindsay, it is not. It is not all right. It is not *fine*.' The last word was spoken in a sneer, a mockery of the times she'd insisted she was.

Lindsay shook her head. 'Antonios, what—'

'When,' he asked, his voice turning savage, 'were you going to tell me?'

Lindsay blinked as he glared at her, his whole body taut with fury, his fists clenched at his sides.

'What…'

'You haven't forgotten, have you?' he enquired silkily. 'The job offer you're so *honoured* to accept?'

Her jaw dropped. 'You read my email—'

'You left it up on the screen. And I'm not going to apologize for some imagined invasion of your privacy when you've been keeping such things from me.' He shook his head, his features twisting with bitterness. 'When were you going to tell me you were leaving, Lindsay, or were you just going to slip away again?'

CHAPTER TWELVE

EVERYTHING IN HIM HURT. Antonios heard his own ragged breathing as he stared at Lindsay and saw the truth in her face. She had deliberately kept the job offer from him.

And why? It felt painfully obvious: because she'd been intending to take it up, to leave him.

Lindsay had gone pale, her breathing shallow. 'Don't have a damned panic attack now,' Antonios growled. 'I won't have an ounce of sympathy for you if you do.'

Her mouth compressed and she swallowed. 'Good to know.'

'Why?' he asked, and heard a world of hurt in his voice, making him cringe inwardly even as fury fired through him. *Theos*, but he'd been here before. Only this time it felt a thousand times worse.

'Why what, Antonios?' Lindsay asked quietly.

She had composed herself, and even that infuriated him. She seemed unaffected by his own agony, but then he hadn't been able to read her before, had had no inkling of the anguish she'd tried so hard to hide.

Perhaps he hadn't changed as much as he'd thought and hoped he'd had.

'Why,' he clarified, 'did you not tell me you had a job offer from a university in New York? A job offer you were thinking of accepting—'

'I haven't accepted it.'

'You're thinking about it, though, aren't you?' Antonios returned. 'In the email you haven't finished the sentence about just what you're *honoured* to do, and why was that? Because you aren't sure.'

Lindsay's face was pale but when she spoke her voice came out calmly. 'No,' she agreed, 'I'm not.'

And somehow her calm admission hurt all the more, and turned his anger into despair. His shoulders sagged and he felt an unbearable weariness sweep through him, making every muscle he had ache. 'And you couldn't even tell me that.'

'I was going to.'

'When?' He shook his head. '*Theos*, what kind of marriage do we have, if we cannot be honest with each other?'

'I don't know.' Lindsay took a deep breath. 'But I'll be honest now, Antonios. I'll tell you exactly what's in my heart because if I don't, I don't think we have a marriage. I don't think there's much point in going on.'

'You always are quick to give up, aren't you?' he said, the words coming out before he could stop them and hitting Lindsay where it hurt.

He saw her flinch but then she composed herself, straightened her shoulders and lifted her chin. 'I'm not giving up. And being honest with you feels like fighting for my marriage, Antonios. For us. It would be easier in some ways to just ignore the things that are hurting you, pretend everything is fine. I did it before, and I'm not going to do it again. Because I love you. Because I want our marriage to succeed.'

He shrugged her words aside, too raw to do anything else. 'So, tell me then. Be honest about whatever it is you have to say.'

'Receiving that email made me realize that I do miss being part of an academic community,' she began. 'Teaching seminars, talking to people who are excited about what I'm doing. But I also knew that I'd committed myself to you, and your life is here in Greece.'

'Such a dilemma,' he cut in, his voice sharp with sarcasm, and she stared at him.

'Are you even going to try to understand?' she asked, and inwardly Antonios cringed.

He was lashing out because he was afraid Lindsay was going to leave him. Just as she'd once been afraid he would leave her. *Theos*, the things you did out of fear.

'I'm sorry,' he said. 'I shouldn't have said that. Please, continue.' He swallowed hard, jammed his hands in his pockets and forced himself to listen without speaking. But if she told him, in that calm and cool way of hers, that she was *leaving*…

'When you brought me to Greece, Antonios,' Lindsay said quietly, 'I was unhappy. So unhappy I didn't notice, didn't even consider, that you were unhappy, too.'

He stiffened, thrown by the sudden change in subject. 'What are you talking about—?'

'I'm talking about how you don't sleep at night. How the moment you drive through the estate gates your whole body tenses and a shadow comes over your face. How you work so hard but you don't even seem to enjoy it.'

Each word felt as if she were stripping him bare, flaying him. He stared at her, shaking his head. 'You're reading too much into something that is temporary…'

'What's temporary, Antonios? This bitterness between you and Leonidas? That's been going on for years. The stress and strain of your job? I see it now and, looking back, I should have seen it before. You weren't just blind to my anguish, Antonios. I was blind to yours.'

Anguish. The word captured him, felled him. Because he knew she was right and he hated it. Hated it because it meant he'd failed.

'I don't see what any of this has to do with your job offer,' he said finally, his voice flat.

'Because when I read that email I thought of you. I thought of us and how maybe we would be happier, you would be happier, away from here. Away from Marakaios Enterprises.'

Emotion leapt inside him but he refused to name it. 'That's a very convenient justification for following your own desires.'

'Tell me you're happy here, Antonios,' Lindsay answered. 'Tell me you don't want to leave. Tell me this is what you want for the rest of your life.'

'I have no choice,' he said, the words torn from him. 'Don't you see that? My father named me as his successor. This is what I was born to do, what I have to…' He broke off, his chest heaving, his fists clenched.

'Who says?' Lindsay said quietly. 'Why can't you control your own destiny, choose your own life? And choose one that makes you happy?'

'There is such a thing as duty.'

'There is also such a thing as your brother,' Lindsay reminded him. 'Someone who wants more authority, who is already working for—'

'*Theos*, enough.' He flung out a hand to stop her from saying any more. 'Happy or unhappy, my life is here. It has to be here. But if you choose not to share it, then tell me so.'

'I want to share it,' Lindsay answered, her voice trembling. 'Of course I want to, but you don't want to share it with me.'

'Not this again—'

'Of course *this* again! You're unhappy, Antonios, but you won't tell me why. You won't tell me what is going on with your brother, or what happened with your father, or anything. How can I help? How can I be your wife, supporting and loving you, when you deliberately shut me out?' He couldn't answer and she stepped towards him, grabbing him by the shoulders. 'I love you,' she told him fiercely, her voice choked with emotion. 'I love you enough to risk everything because I know you can't go on like this. We can't go on. Please, Antonios.' She stared at him, tears running down her face, and the certainty he'd shielded himself with for so long started to crack.

Lindsay had kept a secret from him and he'd felt angry and hurt. Betrayed—as betrayed as when his father had kept the wretched state of the business from him. How could he keep anything from her? How could he perpetuate this life of secrets and lies?

But it's not my secret to tell.

Yet had it been his to keep?

'When I took over the business,' he told Lindsay, the words coming haltingly yet with growing determination, 'I didn't realize—no one realized—that it was in debt. Utterly in debt. My father had a heart attack because he was faced with losing it all.' Lindsay gaped at him and Antonios smiled grimly. 'A shock, no?' he said and she nodded.

'And you didn't tell anyone about this?'

'My father asked, *begged* me not to. Some of his dealings had been…illegal. Criminal.' He drew a shuddering breath. 'Telling my family would have brought such shame to my father. My mother loved him, and my siblings, too. I couldn't bear for their feelings to change, and I knew it would destroy my father. So I worked to get the business back on an even footing.'

She cocked her head, her luminous gaze sweeping slowly over him, and he braced himself to hear recrimination. Rebuke that he hadn't told anyone, that he'd kept it to himself.

'Oh, Antonios,' she said softly, her voice filled with so much love and compassion, 'that must have been so very hard for you. Keeping such a secret for so long, and working so hard.' She shook her head, more tears spilling down her cheeks, and her understanding just about undid him.

'Lindsay, I love you,' he said as he reached for her. 'I know there are a lot of unknowns, a lot of complications, but that is one thing that I know. One thing that it is certain. It is my rock.'

Another tear snaked down her cheek. 'It's my rock, too,' she whispered. 'Loving you. Knowing you love me.'

He drew her to him, needing to feel her soft, slender body against his. 'Then we'll work the rest out,' he murmured against her hair. 'Somehow we'll work the rest out.'

'Antonios.' She pulled away from him. 'It's not that simple.'

'It can be—'

'No,' she answered, 'it can't. I wish it could

because it would make things so simple. Just sail along on the certainty of our love.' Her mouth twisted wryly. 'But it's not simple, Antonios. Your mother said it was endlessly complicated. And love is hard work.'

He stiffened, not wanting to hear this and yet knowing in his gut she was right. 'So what are you saying?'

'I'm saying you need to talk to Leonidas. You need to think about what would make you happy, and how our marriage can thrive.'

He tensed, withdrawing from her. 'Is that an ultimatum?'

She stared at him sadly. 'Does it need to be one?'

'This is about your job offer, isn't it?'

'No, Antonios.' Lindsay shook her head. 'It's about so much more than that.'

Anger fired through him, coming so quickly on the heels of the love and gratitude he'd felt. 'Lindsay—'

'I'll refuse the offer if you want me to,' she told him quietly. 'This is about you. And me.

Us.' She stared at him steadily. 'I wish you could see that.'

And he could see it, Antonios realized. Of course he could. He just hated the thought. He stared at her, the sadness turning down her mouth, the love still shining in her eyes. He hated that he'd made her so unhappy. Again.

'I need to be alone,' he said abruptly and turned from the room.

He walked the length of the estate, ending up in the olive groves, memories of his childhood dancing through his mind. Memories of walking there just a few short weeks ago with Lindsay, when they'd forged this new and fragile foundation of their marriage. He'd fallen in love with her all over again these past few weeks. She'd made coming back here, dealing with Marakaios Enterprises, bearable.

And do you want more from your life than bearable?

Antonios pressed a fist to his forehead and closed his eyes. Lindsay was right. Marakaios Enterprises had been slowly strangling him for a decade. Not just the secret he'd kept from his family, but the whole of it. He was reaching his breaking point and only Lindsay had seen it. Had possessed the courage to confront him.

He would be no less brave. Resolutely, he went in search of Leonidas.

His brother was not in the main villa or his own house; it took Antonios a few stunned seconds to realize Leonidas had gone to the office, on today of all days.

It was dark, twilight having descended without his even being aware of the descent into night, and a few stars glimmered close to the horizon.

A single light shone from the office building. Antonios thumbed the key code and stepped inside. He paused on the threshold of Leonidas's office, taking in his brother's bent head, one hand raked through his hair, the determined yet slumped set of his shoulders.

'It's a little late to be working,' he said quietly and Leonidas looked up, startled, before he gave a shrug.

'The world doesn't stop, even for a funeral.'

For a second Antonios wanted to berate his brother for his callousness, but then he saw the grief in Leonidas's eyes and realized this was how he coped. He was, Antonios thought wryly, starting to see people a little more clearly, thanks to Lindsay.

He took a step into the room. 'I want to talk to you.'

'Oh?' Leonidas eyed him warily. 'About what?'

'About Father.'

He'd spoken quietly, but the two words seemed to bounce around the room, echo in the stillness. Leonidas glanced down at the papers he'd been studying, needlessly rearranging a few.

'What about him?' he asked finally.

Antonios took a deep breath, then plunged. 'Father was deeply in debt, Leonidas. He'd nearly lost it all when he had the heart attack.'

Leonidas's jaw dropped, just as Lindsay's had done. Wearily, Antonios explained it all again: the debt, the shame, the secret.

After a long, taut moment Leonidas pushed away from the desk, turned towards the window. 'You should have told me.'

'I didn't feel I could.' He sounded, Antonios realized, just as Lindsay had when she'd explained why she'd left without an explanation. They were so alike, and yet in such different ways. And they'd taught each other so much. Helped each other so much. 'I realize now,' he told Leonidas, 'I may have been wrong.'

'May have been?'

Temper flared at his brother's obvious sarcasm, but he suppressed it. 'Leonidas, Father made me promise not to tell. He was deeply ashamed that he'd let it get so far. Telling anyone would have felt like a betrayal. It still feels like one now but I recognize that you deserve to know, perhaps more than anyone.' And at least, Antonios thought, his mother had been spared the knowledge of her husband's criminal folly. It was a small mercy.

'I wish he'd told me,' Leonidas said after a long moment. His voice sounded thick. 'I wish he'd seen how much I loved the business, how much I wanted to share it with him. I wish he'd trusted me with that burden.'

'I wish it, too,' Antonios answered. 'I wish there had been no secrets between anyone, ever.'

They were both silent, and then Leonidas

looked up and asked, 'So what now? Things will continue on as usual? You'll give me a little more freedom?'

He sounded so cynical, so jaded and yet also despairing, and Antonios knew it was his fault his brother was like that. He'd given him a very short leash.

'No,' he said slowly, and Lindsay's words echoed through his mind. She'd understood him better than he'd ever understood himself. 'That's not what's going to happen.'

Leonidas let out a bitter laugh. 'I see.'

'No,' Antonios said, 'I don't think you do.' He took a deep breath. 'What would you think,' he asked, 'if you became CEO?'

Lindsay paced her bedroom for an hour, until she feared she'd wear down the carpet with her restless tread. It was evening, and everyone from the reception after the funeral had gone. Parthenope would be leaving to return home tomorrow, and the house, Lindsay supposed, would settle into a new and unwelcome normal.

And what about her and Antonios?

She had no idea if he'd accepted or understood what she'd said. No idea if their marriage was teetering on a precipice or about to take off and fly.

She would refuse the job offer, she told herself, as a sign of her faith in him and their marriage. It had been unreasonable of her even to consider it.

Yet her heart still felt heavy as she headed to her study and opened her laptop. The unfinished email was still on the screen where she'd left it, where Antonios had read it. Lindsay scanned the two sentences and then started writing.

I am honoured that you have considered me for this position, but I am afraid that I cannot accept...

'You're not turning down that job, are you?'

Lindsay's hands stilled on the computer keys and then she turned around in her chair, saw Antonios standing in the doorway of her study. He looked both weary and wonderful, and his mouth curved in a slow, tired smile as he took a step forward. 'Because I wouldn't do that, if I were you.'

Lindsay frowned, uncertainty and hope warring within her. 'You wouldn't?'

'No.'

'But…'

'You were right, Lindsay, about everything. About me. About Leonidas. And, most importantly, about us.'

An incredulous smile started blooming across her face. 'What's happened?'

'I told him the truth.'

'Oh, Antonios.' Her smile widened even as she felt the sting of tears. 'I'm proud of you. That must have been hard.'

'It was. But it was also a relief. I suspect you know what that feels like.'

'Yes.' She nodded and he took her hand, drew her up from her chair. 'Thank you for being patient with me,' he whispered against her hair. 'Thank you for loving me the way I needed, even when I didn't think I did.'

'Oh, Antonios.' Her voice was too choked to say anything more, so she just put her arms around him. He held her, stroking her hair, and she pressed into him, revelling in how he managed to make her feel both strong and small.

'So about that job,' Antonios said with a nod towards her laptop. 'What was it exactly, anyway?'

She eased back to eye him warily. 'It doesn't matter—'

'I think it does.'

Unsure of where he was going with this, she gave a little shrug. 'Assistant professorship of Pure Mathematics.'

'Sounds right up your alley.'

'I suppose.' Actually, it involved teaching an advanced seminar on her research topic, but she didn't need to tell Antonios about that. 'I was just about to refuse,' she told him, stopping when she saw he was shaking his head.

'And I told you I wouldn't do that if I were you.'

'Why not?'

'Because I think I fancy the idea of living in America.'

Lindsay's jaw dropped. 'What?'

'Leonidas is now the CEO of Marakaios Enterprises.'

'But...' Lindsay's head spun. No matter what she'd told Antonios earlier, she'd never actually believed he would resign.

'I offered him the position,' Antonios explained. 'I realized you were right, Lindsay. Being CEO of Marakaios Enterprises has never made me happy, and I know it's what Leonidas has wanted. He deserves a chance, and I deserve a chance to try something else. To be happy... with you.'

'You've put so much into it, Antonios,' Lindsay said, marvelling at how much he was willing to give up. 'You *saved* it—'

'And now I'm handing it over to Leonidas. But I'm not leaving completely.' He gave her a crooked smile that felt like a fist reaching down and taking hold of her heart. No matter what the future held, she loved this man. She wanted to be with him. 'I've accepted a newly created position with Marakaios Enterprises,' he explained. 'Head of North America and Investment Management.'

'North America...' she repeated slowly, her mind whirling. 'Investment Management—but I didn't think Marakaios Enterprises even did that?'

'They didn't, but they will, starting with me. I'm opening a new branch of the corporation in finance, in North America. Based in New York.'

She blinked rapidly, shaking her head in disbelief. 'You'd do that for me?'

'I'm doing it for us. Just like you fought for us by confronting me. I didn't want to admit how unhappy I was here. It felt like a betrayal of my father, of my own sense of honour and duty. But you woke me up, Lindsay. You made me realize what I was afraid to acknowledge to myself.'

'Antonios...' Lindsay shook her head, her eyes shining with tears. 'I don't know what to say.'

'Then say yes. Say yes, I'll take the job, I'll go with you, I'll start this grand adventure.' He squeezed her hands. 'Say yes because you love me and I love you and that really is all that matters.'

Just like Daphne had said. Lindsay could almost feel her mother-in-law's presence, imagined her beaming smile. She squeezed Antonios's hands back.

'Yes,' she said.

* * * * *

MILLS & BOON®

Large Print – September 2015

THE SHEIKH'S SECRET BABIES
Lynne Graham

THE SINS OF SEBASTIAN REY-DEFOE
Kim Lawrence

AT HER BOSS'S PLEASURE
Cathy Williams

CAPTIVE OF KADAR
Trish Morey

THE MARAKAIOS MARRIAGE
Kate Hewitt

CRAVING HER ENEMY'S TOUCH
Rachael Thomas

THE GREEK'S PREGNANT BRIDE
Michelle Smart

THE PREGNANCY SECRET
Cara Colter

A BRIDE FOR THE RUNAWAY GROOM
Scarlet Wilson

THE WEDDING PLANNER AND THE CEO
Alison Roberts

BOUND BY A BABY BUMP
Ellie Darkins

0815 Rom LP

MILLS & BOON®

Large Print – October 2015

THE BRIDE FONSECA NEEDS
Abby Green

SHEIKH'S FORBIDDEN CONQUEST
Chantelle Shaw

PROTECTING THE DESERT HEIR
Caitlin Crews

SEDUCED INTO THE GREEK'S WORLD
Dani Collins

TEMPTED BY HER BILLIONAIRE BOSS
Jennifer Hayward

MARRIED FOR THE PRINCE'S CONVENIENCE
Maya Blake

THE SICILIAN'S SURPRISE WIFE
Tara Pammi

HIS UNEXPECTED BABY BOMBSHELL
Soraya Lane

FALLING FOR THE BRIDESMAID
Sophie Pembroke

A MILLIONAIRE FOR CINDERELLA
Barbara Wallace

FROM PARADISE...TO PREGNANT!
Kandy Shepherd